T0333798

Hugh Mackay is a social psychologist, researcher and bestselling author. *The Question of Love* is his eighth novel.

His non-fiction includes social and cultural analysis, psychology and ethics.

He is a Fellow of the Australian Psychological Society and of the Royal Society of New South Wales, and was appointed an Officer of the Order of Australia in 2015. He lives in Canberra.

Also by Hugh Mackay

FICTION
Little Lies
House Guest
The Spin
Winter Close
Ways of Escape
Infidelity
Selling the Dream

NON-FICTION
Reinventing Australia
Why Don't People Listen?
Generations
Turning Point
Media Mania
Right & Wrong
Advance Australia . . .Where?
What Makes Us Tick
The Good Life
The Art of Belonging
Beyond Belief
Australia Reimagined
The Inner Self

The Question of Love

Variations on a Theme

Hugh Mackay

MACMILLAN

Pan Macmillan Australia

First published 2020 in Macmillan by Pan Macmillan Australia Pty Ltd
1 Market Street, Sydney, New South Wales, Australia, 2000

Copyright © Hugh Mackay 2020

Chapter opener images from 'Goldberg Variations', J. S. Bach,
first edition published by Balthasar Schmid ca.1741.

The moral right of the author to be identified as the author
of this work has been asserted.

All rights reserved. No part of this book may be reproduced
or transmitted by any person or entity (including Google,
Amazon or similar organisations), in any form or by any means,
electronic or mechanical, including photocopying, recording,
scanning or by any information storage and retrieval system,
without prior permission in writing from the publisher.

 A catalogue record for this
book is available from the
National Library of Australia

Typeset in 12.5/18.5 pt Adobe Garamond Pro by Midland Typesetters, Australia
Printed by IVE

The characters in this book are fictitious and any resemblance
to real persons, living or dead, is purely coincidental.

Variations on a Theme

This, which is a dinner of one sort of fish served up in many courses with different cooking and sauce, is one of the very earliest instrumental forms. It has, from the sixteenth century onwards, been used by every great composer, is still popular, and seems likely to go on forever. It has been the medium for some of the most trivial human expression and some of the deepest.
A tune, or 'subject', is given out in all its simplicity, and then repeated many times with changes such as do not conceal its identity, though in more modern examples, it is an identity of spirit rather than of body.
Percy A. Scholes, *The Oxford Companion to Music* (1938)

*

'Variations on a theme' is my favourite musical form – think Bach's 'Goldberg Variations', or the third movement of his piano concerto in D major (itself adapted from a violin concerto); Mozart's 12 variations on a French nursery rhyme . . . As Percy Scholes noted, practically every composer has had a go at it. *The Question of Love* is my attempt to transfer that musical form to the written word.

Hugh Mackay

To Sheila

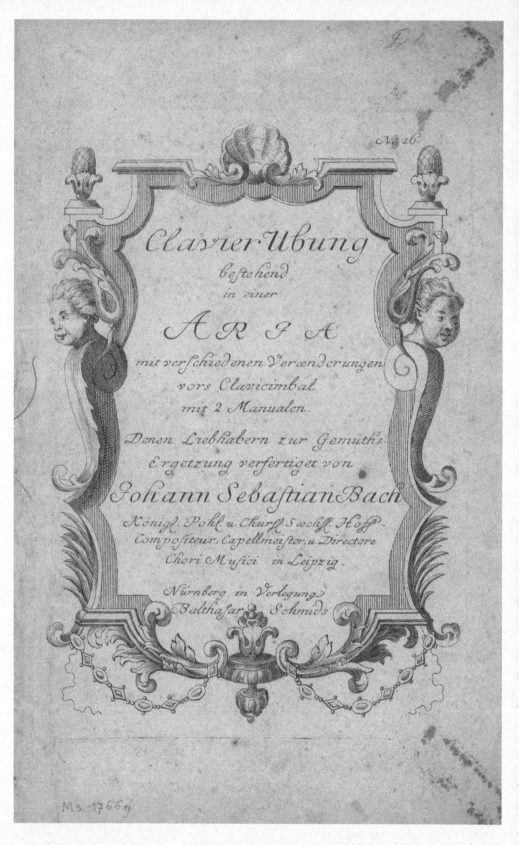

Clavier Ubung

bestehend

in einer

ARIA

mit verschiedenen Veraenderungen

vors Clavicimbal

mit 2 Manualen.

Denen Liebhabern zur Gemüths.

Ergetzung verfertiget von

Johann Sebastian Bach

Königl. Pohl. u. Churfl. Saechfl. Hoff-

Compositeur, Capellmeister, u. Directore

Chori Musici in Leipzig.

Nürnberg in Verlegung

Balthasar Schmids.

Ms. 17669

CONTENTS

1

Coming Home

The sight of his travertine-paved convivium gladdened Richard's heart, as it always did when he came home. Freya was sitting at the farmhouse table they had imported from France, with her back to him. Richard thought her shoulders gave a little shiver as he entered the convivium, but she appeared to be bent over her iPad, so perhaps she was merely responding to something on the screen.

'Home is the sailor, home from sea, and the hunter home from the hill,' he said, removing his linen jacket and draping it carefully over the back of a chair.

His wife looked up at him and smiled. 'Hello, sailor,' she said.

'You okay, Frey?' Richard asked as he kissed the top of her head.

'I'm fine. Why do you ask?'

'I thought I saw a bit of a shiver as I came in. Can I fetch you a sweater?'

'No, I'm fine. It's not cold. Would you like a drink? Or tea? Have you eaten?'

'Yes. Well, no, not really. I had a late lunch with Briggs. I probably drank more than I should have, but so did he. The food was good.'

'Where did you eat?'

'Beppi's. Where else?'

'So, do you want something to eat?'

Freya, Richard now noticed, was bent not over her iPad but over a music score that was covered in pencil marks. He knew what to say.

'No, you're busy. I'll get myself something. Can I get you anything?'

'I'm fine. I ate earlier. Daniel and I had a bite to eat straight after the rehearsal.'

Freya paused, waiting to see if Richard would ask how the rehearsal had gone, how the work was coming on, or even how Daniel was coping with a new baby in the house. Nothing.

She said: 'There's some lasagne in the fridge. You could heat it up in a couple of minutes. I'm happy to heat it while you change, if you like.'

Freya was wearing the long black skirt she sometimes wore to rehearsals. Richard loved the look of her in it. He loved the silky feel of it. His wife – his *young* wife, he often thought with gratitude – was an endless source of aesthetic and sensual pleasure.

He placed his hands on her shoulders, and she turned to face him. He pulled her out of her chair and embraced her, reaching down to stroke the curve of her hips through the thin fabric of her skirt. She responded with a warm kiss.

They stepped apart and smiled at each other.

'I'll heat the food and pour us both a glass of something,' Freya said.

Richard had to admit – but only to himself – that he enjoyed the idea of Freya preparing his food. He particularly enjoyed the sound of her busying herself in the kitchen when he came home from work. He supposed it was a throwback to something quite primitive. Whatever.

Returning to the table, they raised and clinked their glasses of red wine. 'Cheers!' said Richard. '*Salute!*' said Freya. Richard sat and ate his lasagne while Freya continued to work on the score.

After a few minutes, Freya picked up her glass and the score, excused herself, and retreated to her studio. Through the closed door, Richard could hear the rich, resonant sound of her violin and he reflected, yet again, on what a lucky man he was. Freya was beautiful, talented, successful, far less demanding than the wives of most of his friends – he heard regular horror stories from two of his partners at work – *and* she loved him. It sometimes seemed too good to be true, but he believed it *was* true.

Richard often said to his clients that everything in your home – everything in your life – should be either beautiful or useful, or both. He would never say so to Freya, but, to him, she had always fallen squarely into the 'both' category. On top of everything else, she had a bottom like a peach, played the violin like an angel and had a voice like smoke. He used to compliment Freya on her beautiful hair – a fine, greyish gold that hung loosely about her shoulders – until she pointed out that this was a matter of genetics, not accomplishment, and therefore not deserving of praise. 'Handsome is as handsome does' was one of her favourite aphorisms.

Forty-five minutes later, Freya emerged from her studio and announced that Rondo needed to be taken outside for a pee and a short walk. She offered to do it and asked Richard if he would like to come too.

He glanced at his watch. 'I think I'll get ready for bed, if you don't mind. Early start.'

'That's fine.' Freya ran upstairs to the bedchamber and changed into tracksuit pants and a sweater. At the sound of her taking the leash off the hook on the back of the laundry door, Rondo, asleep on the floor of the convivium, sprang to life and scrambled to the front door, his paws slipping and sliding on the pavers, the tail wagging the dog.

Richard checked his emails, sorted some papers for the morning, brushed his teeth and got into bed. He read for a few minutes, felt drowsy, and rolled onto his side.

When Freya returned, Richard was snoring lightly. She smiled, undressed, and slipped into bed beside him. She, too, read until drowsiness overwhelmed her.

2

Coming Home –
1st Variation – 'Restraint'

The sight of his travertine-paved convivium gladdened Richard's heart, as it always did when he came home. He resisted calling it a kitchen/dining area. He had experimented with 'refectory' before conceding it sounded a touch too institutional, then tried 'culinaire' until he discovered it had been registered as a brand name. Now he had embraced 'convivium' and was encouraging the wealthier clients of Urbanski, the firm of architects where he was a partner, to do the same.

Freya, Richard's wife, was sitting with her back to him at the farmhouse table they had imported from France. Richard noticed her shoulders shaking as he entered the convivium, though whether she was laughing, shivering, coughing or sobbing it was impossible to tell. She appeared to be bent over her iPad, so Richard assumed – hoped – she was merely responding to a message.

'Home is the sailor, home from sea, and the hunter home from the hill,' he said, removing his Zegna linen jacket and carefully draping it over the back of a chair. He almost always said this when he came home. And when he left in the morning, he almost always said, 'Another day, another dollar.' If he happened to be at home when Freya left for a meeting, a rehearsal or a performance with the string quartet she had co-founded with her friend Daniel, Richard almost always said, 'Lay 'em in the aisles.' It was a measure of Freya's devotion – or perhaps merely her patience – that she found none of this tedious. Or never said she did.

She looked up at him and smiled. 'Hello, sailor,' she said.

'You okay, Frey?' Richard asked as he kissed the top of her head.

'I'm fine. Why do you ask?'

'I thought I saw a bit of a shiver as I came in. Can I get you a sweater?'

'No, I'm fine. It's not cold. Would you like a drink? Or tea? Have you eaten?'

'Yes. Well, no, not really. I had a late lunch with Briggs, that developer I'm pursuing. I probably drank more than I should have, but so did he. The food was good.'

'Where did you eat?'

'Beppi's. Where else?'

'Well, there are lots of nice places springing up within walking distance of your office, you know. Sagra, for instance, or Verde. Have you tried Verde? You must walk right past it every time you go to Beppi's.'

'No, I never have. They know me at Beppi's. It's comfortable, I guess. Is that boring?'

Freya shrugged. 'Boring? Only if you're bored. If you're not bored, it's not boring. I guess. I imagine *I* might get bored if I ate at the same place day after day, week after week.' Freya pursed her lips. 'Year after year.'

You might be in a deep, deep rut and not even know you're in it, Freya thought. I might even wonder if you are becoming a bit boring yourself, if I let myself wander down that path. Which I won't.

'So, do you want something to eat or not?' she said lightly, concealing her irritation at Richard's new tendency to say both 'yes' and 'no' in the same answer. 'You didn't say if you wanted a drink.'

Freya, Richard now noticed, was bent not over her iPad but over a score that was covered in pencil marks. He knew what to say.

'No, you're busy. I'll get myself something. Can I get you anything?'

'No, I'm fine. I ate earlier. Daniel and I had something straight after the rehearsal.'

Freya paused, waiting to see if Richard would ask how the rehearsal had gone, how the work was coming on, or even how Daniel was coping with a new baby in the house. Nothing.

She said: 'There's some lasagne in the fridge. You could heat it up in a couple of minutes. I'm happy to heat it while you change, if you like. You haven't said whether you'd like a drink.'

Freya was wearing the long black skirt she sometimes wore to rehearsals. Richard loved the look of her in it. He loved the silky feel of it. His wife – his *young* wife, he often thought with gratitude – was an endless source of aesthetic and sensual pleasure.

He placed his hands on her shoulders, and she turned to face him. He pulled her out of her chair and embraced her, reaching down to stroke the curve of her hips through the thin fabric of her skirt. She responded with a warm kiss.

They stepped apart and smiled at each other.

Twelve years of marriage and she still turns me on like no other woman, thought Richard.

Twelve years of marriage – no baby *yet* – and he still thinks I'm here for the sex, thought Freya.

'I'll heat the food and pour us both a glass of something,' Freya said.

Richard picked up his hand-stitched Slovenian canvas duffel bag and dropped it on the floor of his studio on the way to the bedchamber. He still used the more conventional term 'bedroom' for children's and guests' rooms in the plans he drew for his clients' houses, but had rejected 'master bedroom' as a vestige of male supremacism.

In discussions with their friends on many occasions over many years, Richard had declared that he was a feminist. When Freya accused him once too often of doing or saying something she judged to have fallen short of the gold standard of feminism, he stopped using the term. Why lead with your chin? he reasoned. In the nineties, he had passed briefly through a Sensitive New Age Guy phase but had dropped it when he realised women despised SNAGs. What women wanted, he discovered, was a robust debate about gender issues, not a wimpish acquiescence. Balls still counted for something. But he had noticed that using the term 'male supremacist' still won him valuable points in any discussion of women's liberation.

He had long ago learnt to avoid making any remarks that might betray a sneaking regard for traditional gender roles. And yet, in spite of his vigilance, he found it almost impossible to treat women the same way he treated men, even at work. The truth was that he was edgy around women, especially young and beautiful women.

At home, he was right on board with the idea of sharing the cooking and making the bed, and he was more than happy to load and unload the dishwasher (indeed, even Freya conceded he was better at it than she was: it was a design issue, after all), and to handle garbage disposal and light bulb replacement. But he was grateful for the cleaner and gardener whose work relieved Richard and Freya of entire areas of potentially tricky negotiation. He was also conscious of the fact that, among their friends, parents had a harder time dealing with gender issues than non-parents like him and Freya. You couldn't farm everything out.

In spite of all this, he had to admit – but only to himself – that he enjoyed the idea of Freya preparing his food. He particularly enjoyed the sound of her busying herself in the kitchen when he came home from work. He supposed it was a throwback to something quite primitive. Whatever.

Returning to the table, they raised and clinked their glasses of red wine. 'Cheers!' said Richard. '*Salute!*' said Freya. (She thought 'Cheers' vulgar; he thought '*Salute*' pretentious, though neither ever said so.) Richard sat and ate his lasagne while Freya continued to work on the score.

Twelve years of marriage and we've achieved a level of contentment most couples would envy, thought Richard.

Twelve years of marriage and he still has no idea how the sound of his uninhibited chewing and swallowing offends me, thought Freya. No, she thought, 'offends' is too mild: it infuriates me; it's like sharing a dining table with a piece of efficient but noisy mechanical equipment.

After a few minutes, Freya picked up her glass and the score, excused herself, and retreated to her studio. Through the closed door, Richard could hear the rich, resonant sound of her violin and he reflected, yet again, on what a lucky man he was. Freya was beautiful, talented, successful, far less demanding than the wives of most of his friends – he heard regular horror stories from two of his partners at work – *and* she loved him. As far as he could recall, Freya had never once complained about the hours he kept. (Of course, she herself worked some rather odd hours when performing, to say nothing of the touring.) It sometimes seemed too good to be true, but he believed it *was* true. He didn't care to dwell too much on that smug little shit, Daniel . . .

Richard often said to his clients that everything in your home – everything in your life – should be either beautiful or useful, or both. He would never say so to Freya, but, to him, she had always fallen squarely into the 'both' category. On top of everything else, she had a bottom like a peach, played the violin like an angel and had a voice like smoke. He used to compliment Freya on her beautiful hair – a fine, greyish gold that hung loosely about her shoulders – until she pointed out that this was a matter of genetics, not accomplishment, and therefore not deserving of praise. 'Handsome is as handsome does' was one of her favourite aphorisms.

Forty-five minutes later, Freya emerged from her studio and announced that Rondo alla Turca, their Kangal cross, needed to be taken outside for a pee and a short walk. She offered to do it and asked Richard if he would like to come too.

He glanced at his watch, wrestling with two competing urges. He had an early start in the morning and desperately needed a good night's sleep. But he was also aware from some research he had recently read (he was a founding member of Socially Aware

Architects) that relationships, whether with clients, friends or spouses, needed constant nurturing if they were to survive, let alone thrive. The same article reported that married couples spent, on average, less than ten minutes a day talking to each other, not counting texts or voicemail – nor, presumably, body language or companionable silence. A swift calculation suggested to Richard that, all up, he and Freya had that day spent a total of about four minutes engaged in actual conversation, and most of that was admin. But he had asked her if she was okay when he noticed that little shiver – if a shiver was what it was – and he had reported on his lunch with Briggs. (And, while he was calculating credit points, he also recalled that he had made an explicit offer to prepare his own dinner.)

'I think I'll get ready for bed, if you don't mind. Early start.'

'That's fine.' Freya ran upstairs to the bedchamber and changed into tracksuit pants and a sweater. She might once have been disappointed at Richard's decision not to join her, but now she was conscious of a response more like relief. At the sound of her taking the leash off the hook on the back of the laundry door, Rondo, asleep on the floor of the convivium, sprang to life and scrambled to the front door, his paws slipping and sliding on the pavers, the tail wagging the dog.

Richard checked his emails, sorted some papers for the morning, brushed his teeth and got into bed. He read for a few minutes, felt drowsy, and rolled onto his side.

When Freya returned, Richard was snoring lightly. She smiled approvingly, undressed, and slipped into bed beside him. She, too, read until drowsiness overwhelmed her.

3

Love at First Sight

People think there's nothing quite like a string quartet to add class to any occasion – a wedding reception, a conference dinner, a fiftieth birthday bash.

Pity the poor players. It has to be a largish function to warrant hiring us, and that means the noise level will be so high hardly anyone will hear us. We could just as easily be sawing away at fake instruments.

A few enthusiasts will position themselves close to us, nodding and smiling appreciatively, and tapping the fingers of their free hand against the back of the hand holding their drink, in a feeble attempt to simulate applause. Just throw money, we're tempted to say.

We only do it for the money, obviously. And the exposure. We're not naive enough to think we're providing musical uplift or inspiration, let alone education. In fact, even the groupies only seem really responsive when we play their most familiar favourites. The 'Largo' from Handel's *Xerxes* – that gets an occasional smile of recognition. We have a transcription of Schubert's *Trout* piano quintet for four strings. Likewise, the Beatles' 'Let It Be'. And Daniel has done a terrifically lush, quasi-Romantic arrangement of 'Waltzing Matilda' that makes people laugh when they eventually get it. Cutting-edge it ain't. We wouldn't dare play our normal repertoire at those gigs.

When we received an invitation to play at an end-of-year party for an outfit called Socially Aware Architects, Jean-Pierre thought it must be a hoax. 'There *are* no socially aware architects,' he declared bitterly, having recently been ditched by a beautiful young Australian architect. Daniel thought it sounded funny enough to be real, and Olivia and I were in the mood to accept whatever was on offer. It had been a lean year.

The invitation came via our agent. (Yes! We had just acquired an agent!) Once we'd agreed to do it, the agent set it all up, so we had no clear idea of what to expect. We turned up at the venue – the Museum of Sydney – at six o'clock for a warm-up before the guests started arriving at six-thirty. The acoustic was brilliant when the place was empty.

In they came, looking like a bunch of socially aware dentists, socially aware nuclear physicists, socially aware anythings – or, for that matter, socially *unaware* anythings.

When Richard came up the stairs, I knew he was the man I would marry. No question. I didn't even contemplate the possibility that he might already be married. Does that sound melodramatic? Foolish? Inconceivable? Love at first sight – *absolutement!*

I knew he was an architect, of course, and that appealed to me more than the idea of, say, a corporate lawyer or a hedge fund manager. I knew he must be 'socially aware', which sounded positive, whatever it might actually mean. But there he was, bounding up the stairs like a gazelle in a beautifully cut suit, with a lock of thick dark hair falling over his forehead. He was wearing a tie – most of the men weren't – and I remember thinking how distinguished he looked, how confident, and how incongruous the tie was. It featured a cascade of musical instruments tumbling over a navy background. Not incongruous at all, you might think, given he was the guy who had booked the gig, though I didn't know that at the time. It looked comical, somehow, in the context of his immaculate presentation. I'd have thought regimental stripes.

I was mesmerised. (There are times when I still am, all these years later.)

He came straight over to us and waited, with that faraway look I now know so well and understand so keenly, until we had finished the piece we were playing. Then he introduced himself as the person who had invited us to play at the event. He was equally charming to each of us, but he asked if he could have a word with me during the break for the formalities.

That's when he told me he had seen me play at an event three months ago and had been determined to book us for this function. I remember noticing that he said he'd *seen* me play. I had no doubt that he would ask me to join him for a drink after the event.

But he didn't.

He called me the next day, though, and told me he was going to Europe over Christmas and New Year and would contact me to 'arrange something' when he returned in mid-January.

He courted me as if it were the nineteenth century, except for going to bed together at his house on our second date. He came to every single one of my gigs, and we were married the following September. I was twenty-seven; he was forty-two. My friends said it would never last.

4

Coming Home – 2nd Variation – 'Tiles, Tables, Taps'

The sight of his travertine-paved convivium gladdened Richard's heart, as it always did when he returned home.

Freya was sitting at the refectory-style table they had imported from France at vast expense and against Freya's better judgement. But she had been a good sport about it. She had long ago decided that Richard's obsession with the house and everything in it was not worth resisting: there were more important things in her life than tiles and tables. Or, indeed, taps: the time Richard seemed willing to devote to the selection of taps – for their own home as well as his professional projects – astonished her.

Freya's back was to the door, and Richard noticed her shoulders were shaking.

It was a tricky moment for both of them. She had not heard him come in, and so she was caught off-guard: she wished he had not seen her trembling, though it had been involuntary. He, meanwhile, was not in the mood for a deep-and-meaningful, and he knew Freya was in a fragile state. He wasn't sure he wanted to provoke any soul-searching, not after such a heavy day, but he could hardly ignore a signal like that.

'You okay, Frey?' he said as lightly as he could, as he kissed her on the head.

'I'm fine. Why do you ask?' Freya immediately wished she'd left it at 'I'm fine'.

So did Richard. Now he felt an obligation to proceed.

'I thought I saw a little shiver as I came in. Are you cold? Can I fetch you a sweater?' *Little* shiver. Minimise it. 'Cold' was the response he was hoping for; that would be the easiest pathway out of this.

'No, I'm fine. It's not cold. Well – no colder than it usually is on these tiles. Will we never find a suitable rug?'

Richard now mildly regretted having opted for 'cold' – the tile/rug issue had been done to death, in his view – but he could hardly have said, 'Are you upset about something?' without the risk of opening the floodgates.

Richard was becoming sensitive to Freya's reliance on 'fine' as a catch-all response. Angelina, his daughter from a previous marriage, had gone through a phase of saying 'all good', mindlessly, tonelessly, in response to almost any enquiry, and Richard had found that intensely irritating. Freya's 'fine' was pushing him in the same direction.

He noticed she was working on a score. Then he remembered she had been to a rehearsal of her string quartet this afternoon. With Daniel. That damned Daniel and his new baby. His new bouncing baby boy. His new bouncing baby boy with the cute dimples. His new bouncing baby boy with the IQ of a zillion. Better not to mention the rehearsal. He couldn't trust himself to be appropriately restrained, nor to affect the appropriate level of interest if yet another photo of Daniel's baby was shown to him. The smartphone had its drawbacks.

'Would you like a drink? Have you eaten?' Freya asked.

As there was no evidence of food being prepared, Richard could only conclude that Freya had already eaten. With Daniel the cellist, no doubt, but perhaps Olivia the viola player as well. (As if.)

'Yes. Well, no, not really. I had a late lunch, but I wouldn't mind something.'

'There's lasagne in the fridge. You could warm it up in a few minutes. I'll do it for you if you like, while you change.'

Freya knew how much Richard liked to be waited on when he came home late. She knew he was tired. He hadn't acknowledged that she might be tired, too, but that wasn't unusual. He thought being a musician was not proper work. He wouldn't express it like that, but Freya knew that was what he really thought. Music, to Richard, was a form of recreation. He enjoyed it. He loved hearing – and watching – Freya play. But she often felt it would have been much the same to Richard if she'd been a professional tennis player, or perhaps a gymnast.

She also knew that Richard was wary of her friendship with Daniel. She'd known Daniel since they were teenagers at high school together and the formation of their own string quartet – its latest iteration known as Continental Drift – had been the fulfilment of a dream they'd nursed since way back then.

'You haven't said whether you'd like a drink.'

'That would be lovely. Thanks.'

'Red?'

'Of course.'

When Richard came to the table and she put the lasagne in front of him, she knew she wouldn't be able to stick it out for long. When they were both eating, it wasn't so bad. But when Richard was eating and she was listening, the sound was literally unbearable to her. He sucked, he chomped, he swallowed quickly and noisily, and he scraped that wretched fork against his teeth in a way that set her own teeth on edge. And his jaw clicked like a percussive instrument. She'd raised the subject once and Richard was so offended, so defensive, he made it sound as if she were encroaching on his civil liberties. At such times she was conscious of the fifteen-year gap between their ages. At fifty-four, Richard was already showing signs of the combination of calcification and irritability Freya associated with older men, like her late father – though he had been another fifteen years older again when he died.

She bore the noise for as long as she could, then took her score and went to the studio to run over the part she'd been working on. (Yes, Richard, *working*.)

She stopped playing at ten, summoned Rondo for a walk and asked Richard if he would like to join her. She could see him weighing it up – he felt he should, but he really didn't want to. Freya was perfectly happy to walk the dog on her own; preferred it, in fact. It was a time of head-clearing for her, and she didn't like talking when she walked. She preferred fantasising about the lives being lived in the houses she passed, seen through all the lighted windows and unseen behind all the drawn curtains.

She knew Richard would be asleep by the time she returned, and that was fine by her. They both had an early start in the morning.

5

Beauty and Utility

One of the things I always tell my clients is that everything in their home or office – everything in their *life* – should be either beautiful or useful, or preferably both. I try to live by that rule myself. It applies to architectural finishes, of course, and to furnishings, cars, clothes, luggage, everything. Art is a special case. You might say a painting can be useful in a decorative sense as well as beautiful in its own right, but that's stretching it a bit. Poetry – definitely. My favourite art form. Beautiful in its way with words, and useful for all those compressed insights; that creative blend of disruption and comfort. (I strive for that same blend in my architecture, in fact.) Music – well, yes, it can certainly be beautiful and it can be useful for relaxation, inspiration, entertainment. I always think of music as the most *practical* of the arts, somehow.

Creative artists and performers – now there's a different question. If we value the arts, and no one does so more than I, then the creators and performers are very useful indeed. And some of them are as beautiful as the art they create.

Which brings us to Freya.

I saw her playing with her little group at a function one of our clients held to mark the opening of his new office tower. You can scarcely hear a note anyone is playing at those affairs, but I could see her. Oh, I could see her. Gorgeous. That faint smile. The way she moved as she played. Slim. That soft greyish-blonde hair. The viola player was nice, too, but Freya stood out like a beacon of loveliness.

That was not the occasion for an introduction, but my client supplied the contact details for the group. The Orison Quartet.

That's what they were called back then. Googled it, of course. The name seemed weird. *Was* weird. An orison is a kind of prayer, I discovered. Well, if you draw a long bow – no pun intended – I suppose you could say music is kind of a spiritual thing. Maybe. Sometimes. For some people. Anyway, I convinced Freya to change the name, but that's another story. I gather these musical ensembles are always mixing and matching, changing names and partners.

So I went ahead and set up the gig for our rather splendid Socially Aware Architects' end-of-year caper. It was a very new concept then. Our job is almost done by now – most young architects would probably regard themselves as so socially aware they wouldn't need to join the group. Which is why they aren't joining it, presumably. I imagine they are more socially aware than previous generations. It's an education thing. The environment. Sustainability. Scarce resources. Global warming. All these things throw up their challenges to the socially aware architect, but that should be *all* architects, of course. People say – it's a kind of cliché – that architects don't design buildings for people. Well, who else do we design them for? But that was never the purpose of the group. We weren't trying to make buildings more people-friendly – that's a given, surely. No, we were trying to encourage architects to think on a societal scale, but also to pay more attention to our interpersonal relationships – our social networks: clients, planners and so forth. In the beginning, we were pretty avant-garde. Innovative. Pushing the envelope.

Anyway, back to Freya. That was how we met. I engineered it. I didn't want to scare her off, so I was cautious on the night.

Charming enough, I hoped, but not pushy. I had a bit of a history of scaring off women.

I wanted her to see me in a semi-professional context, to get a more well-rounded first impression of me than would be possible over a cup of coffee or a drink. I was making a brief speech to mark the end of the year, in which I referred to our growing numbers and to the very welcome addition of several women to our ranks. I mentioned our mid-year conference in Prague, and summarised the work we had done in trying to influence the curriculum in architecture faculties around the country. I quoted Frank Lloyd Wright, of course: *The physician can bury his mistakes, but the architect can only advise his client to plant vines.* And I used the old Edwin Lutyens line: *There will never be great architects or great architecture without great patrons.* That always goes down well with clients.

Freya never said what she thought of that speech, and I never asked her. I think she was too swept up in the excitement of the evening.

As soon as I saw her playing again, I knew I had not made a mistake. She was beautiful to look at, to listen to and, I had no doubt, to have and to hold.

I gave her a kiss on the cheek – nothing more – and sent her flowers the next day. I had to leave soon after for a Socially Aware Architects' European study tour that was to include Christmas decorations on commercial buildings, so I called Freya to assure her I wanted to see her on my return. Which I did.

At that stage, marriage hadn't entered my mind. On the contrary. Been there, done that, bought the T-shirt, as the young say. I had Angelina to contend with, and the divorce from her mother was painful, acrimonious and damned expensive. I wouldn't have stayed with that woman under any circumstances – she was neither beautiful *nor* useful, as it turned out, though she had a rather brittle prettiness that drew men in. But I admit I did occasionally wonder whether divorce was the best answer. *Damned* expensive.

My ex-wife jumped into another marriage almost immediately – I could have predicted that – but I was determined not to follow suit. There was something rather agreeable about being an unattached and rather successful architect in my thirties, making good money, stashing it away and getting myself into the real estate market as soon as I could. (Given my background, home ownership has always been a matter of the utmost importance to me.) I had plenty of romantic liaisons during that period of my life, but if a woman started to show signs of hankering after wedding bells, let alone babies, I was out of there. I wouldn't call it commitment-phobia; I'd simply say I had an understandably cautious mindset. Once bitten, etc. When I turned forty, I remember wondering if I might ever take the plunge again, but, as I say, the life of the single professional person is a rather agreeable one and I could see no reason to change my status. I think of it as my Velvet Jacket period.

I was certainly not in the market for any more children. Looking back, I was not much more than a child myself – twenty-eight – when Angie was born. The young are far more sensible about parenthood today. At meetings of Socially Aware Architects, we receive regular briefings about the changes reshaping society, and I must say I approve of what I hear about the falling birthrate and the increasing age of new parents. Most first-time fathers today are in their mid-thirties. Very sensible – except for the sleepless nights, I suppose. We have a new father at work who's practically my age, poor bastard. He looks positively haggard.

Angelina was a nice enough kid. But, really, I can't say I'm into young children, to be honest. They don't become interesting until they're well into their teens, and even then it's no sure thing. But I hung in there for a whole year, with the access visits and the holidays and all the rest. Very tough going. The situation was greatly eased when Angie's mother and her new husband announced they were moving to Perth. I think they thought I was going to object, but they misread me totally. Let's just say I didn't object.

By the time Freya and I were married, Angelina was a difficult fourteen-year-old, but things became far less tense with Freya on the scene. Don't quote me, but that kind of thing comes more naturally to women, I believe. I know it's mainly cultural, blah, blah, blah, but I could see it in Freya. She just seemed to know instinctively how to deal with Angie when she came to stay. Both females, of course. It's easier all round now she's an adult: she and Freya get on like a house on fire – let's face it, there's only a thirteen-year difference between them, which can be a bit unnerving in its own way. In fact, I see more of Angie now than I ever did when she was a child. Her mother and what's-his-face always claimed Angie wasn't keen on coming to see me. May I be frank? Back then, the feeling was mutual.

My buildings are my babies.

6

Coming Home –
3rd Variation – 'Flashback'

The sight of the travertine-paved convivium gladdened Richard's heart, as it always did when he returned home. And yet . . .

Pausing at the door, Richard recalled, for the hundredth time, another version of this very scene occurring in another time and another place. He was fourteen, arriving home from school. As he came through the back door, he saw his mother sitting at the kitchen table, her shoulders heaving with terrible sobs. He was shocked, confused, frightened. She had her back to him and he didn't know whether to retreat, in the hope that she had not heard him, or pass through the room saying nothing, or go to his mother and try to comfort her.

There was no precedent. He had never seen his mother cry before. Not once. His mother was famous for her composure.

He waited. It was the most harrowing sound he had ever heard. It was like a wall, with no way through it.

He stared into the room – the shabby linoleum on the floor, the fridge with a rusting hinge, the bare bulb hanging from the ceiling. There had been a light shade, but it had been smashed when, according to his mother, his father had been attempting to kill a mosquito. His father had no doubt been drunk, as he so often was, and angry. He had probably thrown something. At least it had only hit a light fitting.

His father seemed to Richard to be almost perpetually angry, or on the brink of anger. He had once dared to ask his mother why she stayed with him and she had said, with a faraway look, 'He's your father.'

He could never anticipate his father's rages. They seemed unconnected to his own or his mother's behaviour, though for many years he had assumed he was somehow responsible. His mother had reassured him on that point, around the time of his twelfth birthday. He remembered that conversation as the most intimate, the most intense, he had ever had with his mother.

Looking at her now – listening to those racking sobs – he was certain this was about his father. But why at four o'clock in the afternoon?

He must have made an involuntary sound.

His mother turned and saw him standing in the door. She stood and composed herself. Even at fourteen, Richard was amazed by the speed of that transformation. She held out her arms to him. That was unusual – she was reserved as well as composed – and he accepted her embrace with a sense of relief.

As she held him against her tiny frame, there was one more shudder, and then silence.

'Go to your room and change out of your school uniform,' she said, 'and I'll make some toasted cheese sandwiches. We'll have them together on the back porch.'

He did as he was told.

Walking to his bedroom, he was conscious of some shift in the atmosphere of the house. A different smell. A sense of movement. A disruption. Dust in the air.

He glanced into the living area. All the bookshelves were empty. Taking a step inside the room, he saw that his father's beloved sound system had gone. And so had the beat-up old piano on which Richard had so consistently failed to practise that his lessons had been discontinued long ago.

'Mum? What's happened?' His voice came out sounding strangely husky.

'Get changed, Richie. I'm making the sandwiches.'

He went to his room, closed the door, changed his clothes and sat on his bed.

His father had clearly moved out.

His first thought was that there would be no more anger. It didn't occur to him that he might have to see his father again. Regularly. For years to come. Under very different, very strained circumstances.

'Richie?'

His mother's voice was unsteady. He didn't want to upset her. He opened his bedroom door and went out to join her on the back porch. Everything felt strange, dangerous, vulnerable, insecure. He sat down on an old cane chair. His mother was perched on a wooden stool. A teapot, two mugs and a plate of toasted cheese sandwiches – his all-time favourite – sat in front of her on a second stool. There had been a table here when he'd left for school this morning: a table his father had made in woodwork classes at high school. Gone, too.

His mother gave him the bones of the story. She spoke calmly, until she got to the part about them needing to move.

'But why can't we just keep living here?'

When he saw the look on his mother's face, he wished he had not asked. She had crumpled. Had he been older and more experienced, he would have named the look as heartbreak.

'I – we – I will be moving in with Aunty Iris and Uncle Eric.'

'But you *hate* Uncle Eric.'

'Everything has changed, Richie. Your father is starting a new life with someone else. And so are we.'

'Who is Dad starting a new life with? Where?'

'I'll let him tell you all that in good time. It's someone with
. . . money.'

'I don't want *him* to tell me *anything*. I don't want to see him
ever again.'

'You'll feel differently in a little while.'

'But Aunty Iris lives –'

'I know. Wentworth seems a long way away, but Uncle Eric
has arranged a job for me in his accountancy firm, helping out
in the office. The good news for you is that you won't have to
change schools. Grandma Davis has agreed to let you board with
her during term-time, and then you can come and stay in Wentworth for your holidays, if you want to. Your cousins usually go
back there on holidays from their boarding school in Melbourne,
so that could be nice.'

Richard barely knew those cousins – two girls, both older. His
mother had avoided family get-togethers involving Uncle Eric.

'And I'll be able to come to Sydney on the train quite often,
for weekends and special occasions . . .'

His mother's voice trailed away, and there was a long silence.
Then she gave him the saddest smile he would ever see. 'I'm sorry,'
she said, firmly, as if that were her final word on the subject.

'Why do I have to move in with Grandma?' he asked,
conscious that his life had been rearranged for him without a
word of consultation.

'It's all for the best,' his mother said – a line she would repeat
many times over the next forty-eight hours. 'You can stay at the
same school and keep your friends. Isn't that good?'

He thought of Russell, and Geoff, and Barry. He supposed it was good.

'When?' He wanted to talk about something practical. He wanted to know what to *do*.

'I'll take you over to Grandma's this weekend. She's really looking forward to having your company. You'll just have to remember to speak up. Uncle Eric will be here to help us move. We have to be out of this house next week.'

'But I thought this was *our* house.' Richard had occasionally heard his father talk about the struggle to pay the rent, but he had never really processed the significance of that.

His mother shook her head.

'Are you okay, Frey?'

'I'm fine. Why?'

'I thought I saw you shiver as I came in.'

'Oh, I might've. It is a bit chilly. Would you mind bringing me a sweater on your way back from changing? Are you hungry? I remembered you were going to have a proper lunch, so I thought I'd just toast us some cheese sandwiches. Will that do?'

Richard went to his wife, pulled her out of her chair, held her tightly and kissed her with unaccustomed tenderness.

'Perfect,' he said, and she was too astonished to respond.

7

The Pub Test

Freya sat at a table in the bar of The Exchange with her older sister Fern and her younger sister Felicity. The empty fourth chair had been occupied by Richard until a moment ago when he departed in response to a pre-arranged signal from Freya.

She would have preferred to do all this just with Fern, but Felicity got wind of the meeting from their mother and gate-crashed in her usual breezy style.

'Alright, you two – what did you think of him? Give it to me straight.'

'What, no foreplay?'

'Not remotely funny, Felicity. You're sounding more sluttish every time I see you. I won't discuss him at all if you're going to be like that.'

'It was meant as a compliment, dear sister. He's obviously a spunk. I assume you don't just hold hands.'

'Fern?'

'Is the hair dyed, do you think?'

'Yes, I wondered that. It's very black, but he is only forty-one.'

'Is that what he says? I'd have thought late forties, at least.'

'Forty-two next birthday. Which is next week, by the way. I haven't seen his birth certificate, but it all stacks up.'

'He looks quite a bit older than that. Weathered, wouldn't you say? Or is that unkind? Perhaps I should say an interesting face.'

'Interesting, indeed,' said Felicity. '"Victim to the heart's invisible furies", do you think? Has he had his share of invisible furies, Frey?' Felicity was sounding almost solicitous.

Freya and Fern stared in disbelief at their younger sister (half-sister, they both believed).

'Auden,' said Felicity.

'Oh, we know it's Auden. It's just that –'

'I went to school, too, you know.' Felicity folded her arms across her chest and affected a pout.

'Well, he's been married once – briefly – a long time ago. It sounds as if it was pretty awful. Especially the break-up.'

'Children?' asked Fern.

'One daughter. She's fourteen.'

'Ooh. That's not much younger than me!'

'Flick, you're almost nineteen. Nineteen is much, much older than fourteen. I can barely remember fourteen.'

'You're so ancient, of course.'

'Back to the hair, could we?'

'Oh, Fern. Does it matter? You have streaks yourself. Do you think Mike will eventually have second thoughts about you because they aren't natural?'

'Different for men.'

'That's sexist!' said Felicity, ever vigilant on such matters.

'Can't help it, Flick. It's what I think.'

'Anyway, I'm pretty sure it's not coloured. It's always exactly the same. There are no grey roots.'

'No grey roots! Pleased to hear it. Grey roots sound like you'd have to stop to catch your breath every few minutes.'

'Put a sock in it, Flick. You are becoming a very silly, very unpleasant person with a one-track mind. Don't let Mum hear you talk like that. Give Frey a break, will you?'

Freya took a sip of her wine and said: 'So neither my older sister nor my younger sister has anything useful or constructive to say about the new man in my life?'

'That's not fair – I was just asking. About the hair, I mean.'

'*And* you think he's older than he's admitting to.'

'I didn't say that. You asked for a straight response. I thought his voice was very nice. Is he musical at all?'

'Actually, no.'

'No? *No?* What do you mean *no?*'

'He's heard me play – that's how we met. So he *appreciates* music. But he's not what you'd call musical.'

'Never played an instrument?'

'Piano when he was a kid. That didn't last. Typical story. Refused to practise.'

Felicity clapped her hands like an excited child. 'I *love* this! He's on the brink of being, like, geriatric – at least compared to you. And he's not musical. So are we to conclude that it's all about –'

'Choose your words very carefully, Flick.'

'Well, you did warn us he was like a Greek god. I assume you didn't mean a *statue* of a Greek god. The guy *performs*, right?'

'I wish I'd never brought any of this up. Say something, Fern.'

'I must admit the music thing does shock me a bit. I mean, it's practically your whole life, Frey.'

'Yes, and look where living with a musician got me.'

'Well, there are musicians and musicians. I liked Dave, but he was certainly what you'd call an acquired taste. And I don't think a perpetually stoned trumpeter is necessarily the gold standard.'

Felicity suddenly flinched as if she'd been struck. She drew her smartphone out of the back pocket of her jeans. 'Oh. Gotta go, girls. That was a message from Jezza. I thought Dave was awesome, by the way.'

'Jezza? I thought Mum had banned Jezza from the house.'

'Oh, don't worry your head, big sister. He's not coming to the house. He's picking me up outside here in his van . . . like, *now*.'

'I hope you know what you're doing, Flick. Mum has a good instinct where men are concerned, you know.'

'So what are you going to do – tell on me? *Bye-ee!*'

Left alone at the table, the two older sisters rolled their eyes at each other, then Fern rose and went to the bar to buy them each another drink.

'What a relief,' she said as she placed Freya's wine on the table. 'Sometimes I can hardly believe she's a member of our family at all. She drives Mum to distraction, or so Mum says. But there's a really strong bond between them I can't quite read. Like a special obligation. I don't know. There was no way she was going to let me meet Richard without Felicity being present.'

'He's an architect.'

'What?'

'He's an architect. Richard, not Jezza.'

'Yes, you told me.'

'Well, he might not be a musician, but he's sort of arty. Don't you agree?'

'I must say he *looks* like an architect.'

'And what, exactly, does an architect look like?'

'Oh, I don't know. The longish hair. The linen jacket. And, yes, a bit arty, but a bit suave, too. Richard, never Dick or even Rick. Definitely Richard.'

'And?'

'I'd have said he looks . . . *interesting*. I think I said weathered before. Almost – not quite – damaged? But who isn't? A bit distinguished, too, I grant you.'

'A *bit* distinguished? He's drop-dead gorgeous, Fern. I practically swooned when I first laid eyes on him.'

'So you said.'

'Don't you agree?'

'I liked him. Don't get me wrong. I liked him a lot, for a first . . . well, a first look at him. It's just that I've never seen you like this. In such a rush, I mean.'

'I want him, Fern. And I don't want anyone else to nab him first.'

'Second, you mean. I'm glad Felicity wasn't here to hear you say that.'

'He's a good architect, by the way. I've seen some of his work. He's very passionate. Very committed. He wants to revolutionise low-cost housing. Put more style into it.'

'I like the sound of that. He's not a socialist, is he?'

'Believe it or not, we haven't discussed politics.'

'Mike and I talk about little else.'

'Each to his own.'

'You seem so *young* to be falling for a man of . . . let's say forty-two.'

'I'm almost twenty-seven.'

'That's what I mean. Think about it. When you're fifty and in your prime, touring the world with the Orison Quartet, he'll be sixty-five.'

'So?'

'Sounds a bit old, doesn't it? But, look, he might be happy to retire and carry your bags by then.'

'Is that supposed to be a joke?'

'Or stay home and look after the children.'

'Who would, by then, be twenty and not needing to be looked after.'

'So you've discussed children?'

'We have.'

'And?'

'I don't really want to go into it, Fern. Not yet, anyway. You've never discussed your and Mike's plans with me. You didn't say a word until you were well and truly pregnant.'

'Fair enough. It's just that . . .'

'What?'

'Well, it's just that a man's attitude to his own children gives you an interesting insight into the calibre of the man. Wouldn't you say?'

'Not necessarily, no. Circumstances alter cases, Fern. You've always said that.'

'Hmm.'

'Don't go all *hmm*-y on me. Speak your mind.'

'Well, for instance, does he see his daughter? Is he close to her? Is he a good dad?'

'She lives in Perth, so, no, he doesn't see much of her.'

'How does he sound when he talks about her? Or when he talks *to* her on the phone?'

'I really don't want to go into this, Fern. Do you mind?'

'It's just that I remember how heartbroken you were over that last miscarriage.'

'Fern, I'd really rather not go into it. Okay? That was mainly about the End of Dave, anyway.'

'So my opinion doesn't really count?'

'Of course it counts. I was hoping for a kind of blessing, I suppose. I haven't introduced him to Mum yet. And I sort of wish he'd met her before he met Felicity. Anyway, what's done is done.'

'I wonder what he thought of *us*.'

'He loved *you*. Really. I could tell. He was already predisposed, of course. He'd studied your photo. Thought you were like an older version of me.'

'Gee, thanks.'

'As for Flick . . . I probably influenced him too much before he met her.'

'Actually, I thought she was pretty subdued, for her.'

'He couldn't take his eyes off her hair, of course. Even though I'd warned him it's so red it looks fake. And Fern, I'd practically guarantee Richard's hair is not coloured.'

'Don't dwell on it, Frey. What about his teeth?'

'*What about his teeth?* What kind of a question is that? He's not a horse. I haven't inspected his teeth.'

'Are they all *his*, is all I meant. That smile is to die for, I agree. Just wondering.'

'Well, he doesn't take them out at night, if that's what you're asking.'

'Does he always wear those rather tattered jeans?'

'Distressed, if you don't mind. No, he often goes to work in a suit, as a matter of fact.'

'Don't sound defensive. I'm just interested.'

'Well, I'm pleased you're interested. That's a start.'

'It's just that . . . well, I wondered if *distressed* jeans might suit a rather younger person. Frankly, I doubt if Mike would wear pants like that.'

'I agree with you, as it happens. I think Richard was trying to impress Felicity. But those jeans will have to go. He has a perfectly normal pair, as well.'

'One other thing. What is his attitude to his mother? I like a guy to show respect to his mother – Mum always says it's a clue to a man's general attitude to women.'

'His mother died when he was fourteen. He doesn't like to talk about it. Pretty traumatic, naturally, at that age. It happened not long after his father left them, to general relief all round, by the sound of it.'

'Oh.'

'What do you mean *oh*?'

'Just . . . that's so sad. I think I might have been unfair about his looking weathered. Father leaves, mother dies. A fourteen-year-old. Gosh.'

'I agree. Very tough.'

'So . . . this is serious, is it, Frey? I mean, *you're* serious?'

'You could say that.'

'Very serious?'

'Totally.'

'Actual marriage?'

'Absolutely. He only has to ask. And if he waits too long, I'll do the asking myself.'

'Really?'

'Really.'

'But . . .'

'What?'

'You know.'

'I know what?'

'Daniel.'

'Daniel?'

'Yes: Daniel.'

'What in God's name are you talking about? Daniel is one of my oldest and best friends. Period.'

'Period? Really?'

'Really. End of story.'

'That's not what he's been telling Mum.'

'Mum? When does Daniel ever talk to Mum?'

'I'm not supposed to tell you this, but he dropped in on her last week.'

'Go on.'

'I'm not supposed to say anything.'

'Fern, tell me what the fuck Daniel said to Mum.'

'Surely you can imagine. That he was still in love with you even though he was living with Lizzie and their baby. That he believed you were secretly still in love with him, but you couldn't admit it. That he needed to know how serious the Richard thing really was. That he would still be your friend, no matter what. That he had always felt part of our family. Mum was in tears telling me. She loves Daniel. You know that.'

46

'The Richard thing? She said *the Richard thing*?'

'I'm paraphrasing.'

'I'll go and see Mum straight away. Finish your drink. Why are you drinking, anyway? Aren't you supposed to be pregnant?'

'This is my last one. Really.'

'Like hell it is.'

'Frey, you must not talk to Mum about this. Ever. My reputation with her will be trashed if you say a single word about it. I'm telling you because I tell you *everything*. But I promised Mum I would keep this to myself. She was so distraught. She just had to tell me.'

'Distraught? A minute ago she was just in tears and now she's distraught! God, Fern, this is hopeless. *Hopeless!* Oh, this is typical Daniel. Driving a wedge between me and my own mother. Or trying to. He can be a real little shit sometimes. Will Mum say anything to me about it, do you think?'

'Probably not. Definitely not, I'd say.'

'But how can I confront Daniel if I'm not supposed to know?'

'You *don't* know. Frey, listen to me. Read my lips. You. Don't. Know. Okay?'

'So Daniel has managed to top up Mum's already deep well of sentimental tosh about him and me. Planted the idea that I'm abandoning him for "the Richard thing". This is unspeakably awful, Fern. Unspeakably awful and desperately unfair. I don't know what to say.'

'Yes you do. Nothing. *Nothing at all.* Not to Mum. Not to me. Not to Daniel. And certainly not to Richard. Obviously.'

'Have you told Mike?'

'Absolutely not. Nor will I.'

'I hate this. Trust Daniel to do something to spoil the moment. He really is a little shit.'

'Also one of your oldest and closest friends, I seem to recall you saying.'

'I'm going to have another drink, and you can't have one. I'll get you a mineral water and you can bloody well sit there and watch me drink my wine.'

'Oh, by the way, what are you going to get Richard for his alleged forty-second birthday? A ball and chain?'

'Shut it, Fern.'

8

Coming Home – 4th Variation – 'The Joy of Children'

The sight of his travertine-paved convivium gladdened Richard's heart, as it always did when he returned home. Freya, his wife, was sitting with her back to him, and her shoulders appeared to be shaking.

'You okay, Frey?' Richard said as he bent and kissed the top of her head.

There was a distinct pause before she replied: 'I'm fine. Why do you ask?'

'I thought I saw a bit of a shiver as I came in. Can I get you a sweater?'

'No, I'm fine. It's not cold.'

Richard hesitated, not wanting to pry. But he was curious. 'You seemed to be shivering. Are you sure you're okay?'

Another pause. Longer. Freya straightened her shoulders before she spoke.

'Oh, I was probably just laughing to myself. I had a lovely exchange with little Pippa next door when I was coming home. She was sitting on their front steps, waiting for her mum. I said to her, "Isn't it a lovely rainy day?" and she looked a bit puzzled. So then I said, "Listen to the birds. Can you hear them singing? They love the rain, too." We both listened and, sure enough, several birds were trilling on cue. It was a magic moment. Then she asked me why birds sing in the rain – don't you love the questions kids ask? She's only five.'

Richard thought he detected a dangerous conversational corner approaching, but decided to stay with the story and see where it led. Where Freya was concerned, an apparently non-threatening *andante* could very easily morph into *appassionato* or even *misterioso*.

'What did you tell her?'

'Because they love splashing around in the rain, the same way they love dunking themselves in our birdbath. They love the feeling of rain on their wings. It makes them feel all clean and fresh.'

'And?'

'She cocked her head on one side and frowned. Don't you love it when little people frown? Do you think it comes naturally, or are they copying their parents?' Pause. 'Richard?'

Richard was on his hands and knees, studying what looked to him like a chip on the corner of one of the travertine pavers.

'Sorry. Do I think what?'

'Frowning. Little kids frowning. Do you think it goes naturally with thinking, or are they just copying?'

'I don't know. Copying, I suppose. At that age. Nothing to frown about, surely?'

'Anyway, guess what she said.'

'Not impressed with your explanation?'

'Not at all. She said she thought the birds loved the rain because they knew it made the trees grow and they needed the trees to live in. Isn't that gorgeous?'

'Lovely. What did you say?'

'I felt a bit inadequate, actually. But I told her I thought she was probably right.'

Richard returned to the problem of the chipped tile, hoping his smile had brought this conversation to a simple, cheerful conclusion.

It had not.

'Have you ever tried talking to Pippa yourself, Richard?'

The tile was not chipped, it turned out: some of the grouting had come away. It was annoying how the best artisans, working with only the best materials, could still fuck up a simple thing like grouting. Or perhaps it was the dog.

'Richard?'

'Sorry. What? Pippa? So she liked the bird thing. That's good.'

'Have you ever talked to her yourself?'

'Who?'

'Pippa. The five-year-old next door.'

'I know who Pippa is. No, I don't think I ever have. I talk to Gavin a bit – when we're putting the bins out, mostly. Why do you ask?'

'My period came today.'

There was a long pause then Richard said, 'Is there a link? Have I missed something?'

Richard had not missed anything. He knew there was a link, but it suited him to slow the pace a bit. Get Freya to be more explicit. Coded remarks were dangerous, in his experience. You assumed you knew what people were driving at, but often you didn't. And vice versa. Better to have it spelt right out.

'I'm talking about children. A child. Our child.'

'Ah.'

'It's not going to happen naturally. That's pretty obvious, wouldn't you say?'

Richard was unequivocally against the idea of children. Well, any more children. But here was Freya, at thirty-nine, unexpectedly mounting a last-ditch assault, and so he had agreed to let nature take its course, being fairly confident that, at this late stage, its course would carry them towards terminal infertility and a life of continued comfort, peace and relative prosperity, disturbed only by occasional visits from Angelina. Freya had had a complicated termination and two traumatic miscarriages before he met her, so her reproductive record was not promising, in his view. It was one of her many attractions; one of the things that had finally persuaded him to marry a second time.

But if it happened, it happened. Freya had said she was perfectly happy to modify her working life to take primary responsibility for the child, if they were 'lucky enough' to have one. She knew Urbanski was on the brink of another growth-spurt and she assured him she would never do anything to jeopardise his role in that. (Richard hadn't wanted a dog, either, but Freya had said she would look after it, and she had been as good as her word on that one, he had to admit.)

'I might heat up something to eat. Would you like something?'

Freya shook her head, determined not to be deflected.

'Can I pour you a glass of wine then?'

'Okay. Yes. Thanks.'

The lasagne was in and out of the microwave in five minutes. The wine was poured, the glasses clinked, and the only words spoken in that time were a muted 'Cheers' and a grimly defiant 'Salute'.

As a form of aural self-defence, Freya took a raw carrot out of the fridge and bit noisily into it. Even as she chewed, she picked up the conversation where it had trailed off.

'Daniel and Lizzie did it by IVF. They had a lot of disappoint-ments along the way and it ended up costing them almost forty thousand dollars, plus a lot of stress. They will be paying it off for years – a mortgage is out of the question. There was also the risk of multiple births, but they got what they wanted. Let me show you the latest –'

Richard held up his forkless hand.

'You've shown me their kid before. Very cute.' Richard said this as lightly as he could. He didn't want to compound this tricky agenda with a further excursion into the life and times of Daniel. (Forty thousand dollars? *Christ!*)

An awkward silence descended on them. Richard wanted to believe the matter would be allowed to rest, at least for the time being. Freya was considering how best to ensure that it would not rest. She had major new ground to cover.

'Do you know about surrogacy, Richard?'

Uh-oh. Time to slow things down again, thought Richard. Ease back. Even let yourself appear a little slow-witted.

'I know what surrogacy *is*, Frey. Of course I do.'

'No, I mean in relation to reproduction.'

Suddenly testy, Richard said: 'You mean like this rent-a-womb stuff we hear about in the media? Illegal, isn't it?'

Tears would flow if Freya let them. But it was important not to let them flow just now. She knew Richard had plenty of evidence for his theory that she was a textbook sufferer from pre-menstrual tension and she could feel, right now, the urge to give way to dramatics. And she could feel that familiar, ferocious conviction gripping her, the conviction that the way she was feeling now – with this monthly tide of hormones washing through her brain – was the way she always *really* felt; it was just that she was less inhibited about expressing it at this time of the month.

'It is illegal here. That's true. But not in other parts of the world.'

They'd often discussed IVF, but, given her history, Freya had herself dismissed it as an expensive experiment that was not worth the risk: 'What if we did achieve a pregnancy and then I blew it yet again?'

'Frey, why don't you tell me exactly what you're thinking, and then we can discuss it rationally.'

Richard had finished his reheated lasagne, belched with scarcely any attempt at suppression, drained his glass and was pouring another. Freya set aside her half-eaten carrot and took a tiny sip of wine. She wanted a clear head for this. Especially now Richard had introduced his favourite word: rational.

She looked at him. A surge of love overwhelmed her. His lush, wavy black hair with its ridiculously distinguished traces of grey now appearing at the temples; his rugged jaw, more suited to a film star than a brilliant architect; his powerful shoulders. She admired his steely determination: this was a man who tended to get what he wanted – including her. Though she occasionally wished for more flexibility, Richard was loyal, mostly kind, and very supportive of her career, even if he only took it half seriously. She knew she wanted to be with him, and no one else, until the day she died.

But her thoughts this night were of life, not death. If she were shopping in a sperm bank, she'd want a father just like this for her child. Eye-wateringly handsome. Clever. Creative. Yes, he could be pompous – she still cringed, all these years later, whenever she recalled his speech at the Socially Aware Architects function where they had met. He could be arrogant, insufferably opinionated and subject to childish sulks. But she wanted his baby. Though it scarcely seemed to make sense to put it like this, she wanted *his* baby even more than she wanted her own.

That, in fact, was her plan. She had lost faith in her own capacity to reproduce and she was frankly scared of the very idea of producing a child from old eggs, even if it were possible. So the solution seemed elegant: Richard's sperm, frozen and shipped to the US; a young donor's eggs used to conceive a healthy embryo in vitro, and the embryo implanted in the uterus of a second woman. Finally, Richard's baby in the arms of Freya, and no one else having any legal claim to be the biological mother.

It was a rational plan. The relationships with both women would be commercial, not emotional, and that should appeal to Richard. Whatever other reservations Richard might have, he surely couldn't deny it was a rational plan.

9

Mother and Daughter

I must say Freya can be disarmingly direct sometimes. Or do I mean 'alarmingly'? Anyway, she burst in here, those blue eyes of hers flashing like a police car, and scarcely drew breath before she tackled me about something I'd said to Fern in the strictest confidence. The *strictest confidence*. So now I can't trust Fern, either.

The thing is . . . well, look, the thing is Daniel. Daniel and Freya. For years I used to say that as if it was all one word. Danielanfreya. They were just so lovely together. Such close friends. You could sense the rapport. And he's such an attractive boy. Really. And so caring. So thoughtful. And so clearly besotted with Freya. *Besotted*. I thought it was a match made in heaven. Both musicians and everything. Similar ages. Similar backgrounds. I've never met the parents, but you can tell. Good manners. I still think that counts for a lot. The little courtesies of everyday life. For a young man, I thought Daniel was quite exceptional in that way.

I don't like to use the word 'sexy', but there it is: he is a very sexy young thing. Anyone would say that. Any woman would. So I thought, well, why not? Frey was young, but it seemed inevitable that they would marry. 'Get together', anyway. Who marries these days? I speak as a widow, of course, though that's a label I'll never get used to.

But, no, typical Freya. That reckless streak. She took up with that dreadful trumpeter. Dave. *God*. I tried to call him David but they all laughed at me. It had to be Dave. *Da-ave*.

Actually, I never lost contact with young Daniel. He was always so attentive. So, you know, affectionate. He confided in me – but not like a mother. More like a friend. When he gave me a hug or a kiss it really felt as if he meant it. You know? It wasn't just perfunctory.

Freya never liked me seeing him when she wasn't present, so I simply stopped telling her. He was very supportive when Frank died. Freya would have no idea of that. And now Charles is – how shall I put this? – back on the scene? *Ugh.* I hate mealy-mouthed talk like that. Anyway, now Charles is becoming a more established part of my life, Daniel is really the only one who knows or understands the depth of it. The girls must have an inkling. I don't try to hide it – I just don't push it in their faces. It's three years since Frank went, so I don't feel there's anything remotely improper about it. But we haven't said anything formal about it. I don't know. I'll just have to judge the moment. Felicity sees him, of course, since she still lives here. Most of the time, anyway. He acts like an uncle to her. Always has. Well, not always. But the other girls . . . no.

Strangely enough, Charles has never met Daniel. I like to keep it that way, for some reason. They each know about the other, but why complicate things? They'd have nothing in common, and I don't need any more strain in my life.

So. Freya's visit. She stormed in here – only the most cursory glance at the pair of new curtains I've hung in the breakfast room – and got straight into it.

'Why have you been talking to Daniel about Richard? What did Daniel say about him? What did *you* say about him?'

I was taken aback, I don't mind admitting. If only Freya knew the context – the many hours I've spent with Daniel going over what happened between them, encouraging him to be bolder – and then, when Lizzie and the baby happened, trying to let him see that we could still be friends. And that he could still be friends with Freya, obviously. They work together, after all. Keep the channel open: that's what I always say to him. You never know, I always say.

I refused to react. Freya doesn't listen when she's in that sort of mood. I told her Daniel and I were good friends and that he sometimes came to me for advice about the baby. That's almost true. She didn't like that. Not one bit. She didn't like to be reminded that Daniel and I have a relationship independently of her.

'Daniel is a little shit, Mum. A little *shit*.' I distinctly remember her saying that, because it is so obviously untrue and she so obviously doesn't believe it herself. Also, the language. *Ugh*. We don't talk like that in this house. Well, I don't. Never have. Frank was very strict about language. Swearing. *Very* strict. Even Felicity – she of the foul mouth – was careful around Frank.

'And Richard is the man I intend to marry. *Marry*. For *life*. Do you understand? He is not to be the subject of idle chat between you and the deeply delusional Daniel.'

Deeply delusional. I recall that bit, too.

I said, as simply as I could, that I thought Daniel was still in love with her and there was nothing amazing or terrible about that. People can love more than one person at a time. Everybody knows that. Daniel certainly knows it. I know it myself.

Then Freya tried to get me to say something positive and supportive about Richard. I hadn't even met the man at that stage, but here she was, expecting me to be all delighted on her behalf. I was prepared to concede that, by the sound of it, he was a decent chap who apparently loved one of my daughters. I could hardly have been expected to offer any more than that, sight unseen.

'Oh, great. "A decent chap". Thank you so much,' she said.

She was rather worked. Very. Said something about wanting my blessing. My *blessing*. Not like Freya at all.

I was tempted to say, 'Well, he sounds like a much better proposition than *Dave*', but I restrained myself.

It kind of petered out then, as if she'd run out of steam. She actually admired the new curtains and even asked me about the arthritis in my hand. (No worse, thankfully.) But that was just the calm before the storm, because she suddenly seemed to go slightly mad. She began shouting at me. 'Are you ever going to admit where Felicity's red hair came from? Did Dad know? Are you ever going to be *honest* with us? About *anything*?'

Then she started sobbing and ran out of the house. It was an astonishing performance. She did ring me later to try to justify her appalling behaviour. I hope I was gracious.

Actually, I've tried to talk to her – to both the older girls – in a sensible way about Charles, but if I happen to mention how well he's done out of novated leasing, Freya simply laughs and claps her hands over her ears. She doesn't even try to understand. Doesn't even try. Look, since I've got to know Richard a bit, I must say I don't mind him. Except he's such a bore. Daniel is more – I don't know – earthy.

Anyway, it's Freya's life. And mine is mine.

Variatio 9.

Canone alla Terza. a 1 Clav.

Variatio 10. Fugetta. a 1 Clav.

10

Daughter and Mother

Ever since I was a little kid, I've known that my mother needed careful handling. Not that she's a prima donna. Well, not exactly. But she certainly likes being the centre of attention – especially with men – and I always felt I was falling short in some way. Even more strangely, I sometimes felt it suited her for me to fall short. She didn't like to be outshone. Very needy, my mother. Dad adored her until the day he died, but that was never enough.

I was an adventurous, impulsive sort of child – climbing trees, crawling into drains, never staying close enough to shore when we went swimming. (I loved swimming almost as much as playing the violin. Still do – my daily swim is as therapeutic as my daily practice.) Mum would often tell me that something I was doing wasn't ladylike. *Ladylike!*

I was right into music, of course, which was never Mum's thing. She didn't disapprove – she just didn't get it. She had clearly hoped I would be an academic star like Fern, and I never was. Neither was Felicity, when she finally came along, but she was a sporty kid and Mum seemed to love the reflected glory of that. (It probably helped Felicity's cause that she was a rather odd-looking child – is that too uncharitable?) But music? No. Zero grasp. I *loved* practising my fiddle and that drove her nuts, too. I never spent enough time doing other homework. If I wasn't practising, I was outside mucking around.

You could say we were never on the same wavelength. I yearned to spend more time with Dad, but he was always busy, often away, and when he was at home, Mum needed his undivided attention.

And then Daniel came along and she was enchanted by him. Even more than I ever was, truth be told. She flirted with him. There was no other word for it. It was excruciating. But he didn't seem fazed by it. I think he believed if he could keep Mum onside that would give him some sort of privileged access to me. Fat chance. Our little fire burnt out very quickly.

But I thought that was all in the past. Then Fern tells me Daniel and Mum have been having tete-a-tetes on the subject of Richard, when Mum hadn't even met him at that stage. That's actually typical of Daniel. And typical of Mum, too. There was no way I was going to let them get away with this. Especially after she told Fern about it.

Knowing Mum, and knowing me, I had to approach this rather carefully. It couldn't seem like an attack, but I had to let her know that I knew about it and that I was mightily displeased. I also thought I might be able to suggest – ever so gently – that her first loyalty should be to Richard, not Daniel. She knew how serious I was about Richard. Even though she hadn't met him I'd probably told her more than she wished to know; probably come on too strong. I do that a bit. I'd certainly hinted that, in my mind, marriage was a distinct possibility.

Anyway, I took a deep breath and knocked on her door. (For some reason, she changed the locks after Dad died and Fern and I were never given new keys.)

She looked gorgeous, of course, in a silk Diane von Furstenberg number. Ash-blonde hair perfectly coiffed. Everything up a notch since Dad died. She always looks gorgeous, as if she's expecting to go somewhere special at any moment, or as if she wants to be prepared for an unexpected caller.

I wasn't unexpected.

'Hello, Mum,' I said, as cheerfully, as normally, as I could. I kissed her on the cheek while she kissed the air. We almost hugged.

I asked about her arthritis. I don't like to think of her in pain – well, not physical pain, anyway. I wouldn't mind if she felt a bit of guilt or shame occasionally. I took her hands in mine and examined them. They looked pretty good. Nails immaculate, naturally.

She mentioned she'd hung new curtains in the breakfast room, so we trooped in there for a close inspection. They were lovely, of course. I told her they were lovely. Even after I'd told her, she asked me if I liked them. We went three times around that loop.

She offered me tea. I accepted, and made it for both of us.

We sat together in the breakfast room. I broached the subject as gently as I could. I mentioned that I'd heard she'd been speaking to Daniel about Richard and I had felt a bit uneasy about what was reported to have passed between them.

'Oh, Fern, then, was it?' She rotated her shoulders back and forth in that way she does to indicate annoyance.

I persisted. 'I gather Daniel is claiming to still be in love with me. Not sure why he would say that, given Lizzie and the baby . . . to say nothing of Richard.'

'And, indeed, we did say nothing of Richard.'

I didn't believe her, of course, but I'll say one thing for Mum: when she tells a lie, she convinces herself it's true and nothing will budge her. The information that Daniel still loves me wasn't exactly news, since he manages to convey that every time we meet, but it was the idea of the two of them discussing me – and Richard, I have no doubt – that galled me. Though here's a funny thing – I have to admit I was more steamed up about it when Fern first told me than I was there and then, sitting in Mum's breakfast room, admiring the curtains and realising she wouldn't have been able to resist another chance to have Daniel to herself – especially if the question of love was on the agenda. Mum is such a *victim* of love. Of the whole *idea* of love.

Really, Daniel was the guilty one. Daniel, the little *shit*. He'd initiated this, for sure. He had the advantage of knowing Richard, so he'd have been trying to turn Mum off him before she'd even met him. He'd have thought, in his tiny twisted mind, that if he could convince Mum he was still in love with me, she'd be able to convince me of . . . what? The need to stay single and celibate, so Daniel's fantasies could rage unsullied by an inconvenient truth, like the prospect of me becoming attached to Richard?

The more I looked at my mother, the more pointless and puerile this whole scene seemed to be. I was almost sorry I'd brought it up.

And then she said something that flipped a switch in my head.

'Daniel and I are quite close, you know.'

Daniel and I are quite close. *Quite close.*

Considering how I was feeling at that moment, I think I stayed remarkably calm. For me. I did tell her a few home truths about Daniel, including, I admit, a rather vehement and not terribly kind critique of his skill as a cellist. It was a sort of metaphor for sex, I guess – it came from a very deep place – but Mum would never have cottoned on to that.

Next thing, like an idiot, I heard myself saying something about Charles. Where did that come from? I restrained myself from telling her that Fern and I call him 'the Monk'. (We got there via ranga/orangutan/monkey, and rather liked its ironic connotations.) But I did hint at how insufferably boring we both find him. Him and his fucking novated leasing. (I think I actually uttered the f-word, banned in Mum's house.) I certainly mentioned, not for the first time, that, thanks to her, our family ran on a high-octane blend of secrecy and deceit.

Maybe that's what set her off. Anyway, she started weeping. It was extraordinary. She never weeps. I never saw her shed a single tear over Dad's death. Not even at the funeral. Fern and I did all the crying. Everyone said how remarkably composed Mum was and she took that as a compliment, of course, though I doubt if it was intended as one.

Anyway, there she was: weeping. I never really tried with Charles, she said, as if her determined coolness towards the very idea of Richard – even her initial resistance to the idea of meeting him – was some sort of payback. As if I should make more of an effort to understand the importance of Charles's work; the inherent value to the economy, and to individuals, of novated leasing. *Novated leasing!* (I certainly understand that Charles makes an awful lot of money out of it, whatever it is, and Mum dresses – lives – more extravagantly than ever before.) Suddenly, the focus had shifted from my complaint about her conversation with Daniel, and her attitude towards Richard, to my attitude towards Charles. I was now the guilty party. She has always been good at pulling that sort of switcheroo. Manipulation, pure and simple, and very impressive in its way.

I tried to get back to the main point – the advent of Richard in my life and all the transformations I was certain would follow. I think I might even have shed a few tears of my own at that point. It mattered so much to me – and to Richard – that Mum should be prepared to welcome him into the family. Ours is such a fucked-up family, I don't know why it mattered. But it did, and it still does. I think maybe because Richard's own family fell apart when he was at such a vulnerable age. Even our crazy, secretive, fucked-up version is better than nothing. And I honestly do think we all love each other, in a funny kind of way.

I ended up feeling sorry for my mother that day. It was very fraught. We didn't even say goodbye, though I rang her later and offered a sort of half-apology which she sort of half accepted.

11

Coming Home –
5th Variation – 'A Certain Smile'

My favourite homecomings are those when Freya greets me at the door and unleashes her most uninhibited, her most enchanting smile – a smile that lights up her face and melts my heart, every single time. It's such a welcome contrast from the more usual sight of her sitting at the convivium table, hunched over a musical score or tapping away on her tablet.

That smile. Those bright white teeth, perfectly shaped, perfectly spaced; those full lips, generously parted; sparkling eyes, crinkled nose; the single dimple in her right cheek; chin raised, as if she's expecting to be kissed.

A few weeks into our relationship, I ventured the obvious question: are your teeth completely natural? It didn't go down well. Freya thought I was implying that such perfection could only come from implants or caps. I wasn't actually implying that, but it's true that nature rarely doles out such perfection as Freya's teeth.

Back then, I didn't appreciate how resistant Freya is to compliments on her physical appearance – teeth, hair, skin, earlobes, fingers. She relishes compliments on her accomplishments, but not references to what she regards as the accidents of her genetic inheritance.

Of course, perfection isn't the same thing as beauty – we've discussed that, over the years, though only in the most theoretical terms, of course. (I have learnt something.) The essence of beauty, I've come to believe, lies in the imperfections, the asymmetries that rescue a face, or a building, from blandness and predictability. Moles were not once called 'beauty spots' for nothing. And, in spite of the perfect teeth, there's that single dimple – just one – and a very slight, and very charming, crookedness in the smile itself. (I've kept this observation to myself.) I think it's something to do with the fact that her lips stretch a little further on the right side of her mouth than on the left. Such things interest me: I'm in the beauty business, after all, beauty and utility. The relationship between the two is often mysterious – as it is in this case. This is a smile that is beautiful in and of itself; this is also a smile that *works*.

When Freya smiles, I feel its effect deep within me, beyond conscious thought; like a poem written in light or the wordless songs of angels. I see its effect on others, too – on audiences she plays for, on her mother and at least one of her sisters. On the wretched Daniel, of course.

In performance, her face is intent, focused and impassive. She sways a little as she plays, and it is clear that she is utterly absorbed in her work. But there is no sign of pleasure. One night – I recall it clearly – the audience response was a little tepid. The members of the quartet stood to take a bow and you could see they were a bit crestfallen; a bit disappointed. Then Freya smiled at the audience. Full voltage. The applause grew. People rose in their places. Her colleagues looked at her and then they, too, smiled.

Something happens when Freya smiles like that.

I've seen that smile completely disarm her mother. You'd never say they have an easy relationship, those two. Sparks sometimes fly but, more often, there are sullen silences that I find deeply unnerving. I tend to leave the room. But when Freya is determined either to get the response she wants from her mother or to shut her down, she simply hyper-smiles at her. It happened on one occasion, years ago, when they were discussing Fern's first pregnancy – long desired by the mother, who said she had always wanted grandchildren, and that might be true, but I think she also wanted a symbol of the fact that Fern wasn't going to run off and leave Mike in the way that she had, according to Freya, abandoned several previous partners. For a long time, Freya had thought Fern was a textbook bolter, but the pregnancy – or Mike – had obviously changed all that.

Right on cue, the conversation had swung around to Freya and me . . . and a theoretical 'family'. Perhaps her mother feared that Freya, too, might bolt (I sometimes fear it myself – it's my greatest fear, in fact). Perhaps she feared that I might be the one to go. I know she has never really warmed to me, so 'feared' might be the wrong word. Perhaps she was unnerved by some recent hair-raising chapter in the endless saga of Felicity – or 'Flick' as her sisters insist on calling her – and needed to be reassured that Freya was as settled, as stable, as Fern was turning out to be.

The truth is, Freya is neither settled nor stable. Probably never will be. Her soul is restless by nature. I get that. Music is a balm, not a cure.

Anyway, this particular conversation trundled along its well-worn track, leading inexorably to the moment when her mother asked Freya: 'Do you think music is really the right thing for you? I mean, long term? I mean, as a *career*?' Meaning, of course, that Richard would be quite capable of supporting you and a baby if you decided to stop work for a while; that this fragile so-called career is absorbing too much of your energy and distracting you from the prospect of motherhood; that such an uncertain and erratic professional life is quite unsuited to a baby's demands for routine, reliability, predictability. (Ironic, really, that Freya was so resentful of her mother's cajoling on the subject of babies way back then, yet she is cajoling me in almost precisely the same terms now.)

The argument came to an end quite abruptly when Freya smiled at her mother in a way that conveyed unspoken messages of love, understanding, sympathy, generosity, kindness . . . and please shut up. And that's what her mother did.

Daniel, of course, is a different kettle of fish entirely. I may never know the full story. They were lovers, obviously, when they were very young. He and Freya somehow remained friends – I've never been able to do that with an ex: when it's done, it's done. That's my style; I think I get it from my mother. Freya says she has never felt a flicker of desire for Daniel in all the years since then, and I desperately need to believe her because the alternative would be a shortcut to madness. She doesn't even appear to esteem him very highly as a musician as far as I can tell. I hear her on the phone talking to Olivia, their viola player, and she seems to speak rather disparagingly of his musicianship, though he's obviously reliable. I wouldn't know about any of that, one way or the other: he seems to do a perfectly adequate job, playing his cello and gazing adoringly at my wife. She's the leader, she says, and he needs to look to her for cues. Maybe.

Her version is that they have major differences of opinion over interpretation, and Daniel is often offended by her insistence on doing it her way. I know how he feels, though I have no sympathy for him.

I've seen his theatrics when they have occasionally rehearsed at our place. I've seen him sulking. Moody. Surly. Unresponsive. And I've seen his spirits lift in an instant when Freya has turned and smiled at him. Right at him. Full on.

Those bright white teeth, perfectly shaped, perfectly spaced; those full lips, generously parted; sparkling eyes, crinkled nose; the single dimple in her right cheek; chin raised, as if she's expecting to be kissed. (But not by Daniel; please, not by Daniel.)

12

A New Client

The new client had sounded impressive on the phone. Strong. Rational. Realistic. Articulate. Clear about what was wanted. Richard loved the challenge of renovations. Creation was every architect's chief passion, but Richard saw renovation as a kind of transformation – just as creative, in its way, as starting from scratch. And, in any case, we never really start from scratch, he often told his colleagues: there's always a streetscape, or a land-scape, or a plot of land with its own character, its own demands. We always start with *something*.

This project sounded both challenging and lucrative: getting some character into what sounded like a pretty charmless house. It could hardly have been further from Richard's real passion – creating stylish low-cost housing – but he was realistic enough to know that the domestic side of Urbanski depended on its high-end clients.

As he usually did when he was making his first visit to a prospective job, he parked well away from the site and strolled up and down the street to get a feel for the context. It was a leafy street, typical of the affluent Upper North Shore, about as far as you could get from Richard's comfort zone in the trendy Inner West. Bush could be glimpsed through the gap between some of the houses – they apparently backed on to some kind of nature reserve – and he had to admit there was an air of gentility about the homes themselves, mostly two storey.

Except number twenty-four. Single storey. Hard to think of any way to describe it except as a stock-standard triple-fronted brick bungalow. It was in good enough nick, but somehow managed to look as if it were in the wrong street. Expensive, but dreary. Almost neglected. The few straggly shrubs in the front garden contrasted with the lush, well-tended gardens on either side.

There was, improbably, an Aston Martin parked in the driveway, as if on show.

Richard returned to his car and drove back to the house. He grabbed his duffel bag containing notebook, tape measure and iPad, walked up the drive – on closer inspection, the Aston was far from new – and knocked on the door.

There was a long delay before he heard footsteps approaching and a short, stocky man clad in an immaculate suit, complete with silk tie, appeared at the door, holding two glasses of champagne.

'You must be Richard,' he said, holding out one of the glasses.

'And you're Lincoln, obviously.' They smiled at each other, clinked glasses, and shook hands.

'Come in, come in,' said Lincoln. 'Looks a bit of a hovel, but that's precisely why you're here. Dehovelisation. I'm told you're the best there is.'

Richard glanced around dubiously. If they had the money for the sort of renovation Lincoln had been talking about on the phone, it wasn't evident in the state of the interior. Perhaps they had bought cheaply with the intention of tearing the place apart. A more typical client might have preferred to knock it down completely and start again.

'Living the dream, are you, bro?' said Lincoln, exuding good cheer.

Richard wasn't sure how best to respond, so he grinned and said, 'I do my best.'

Moving briskly, almost excitedly, from room to room, Lincoln painted a vivid word picture of his own dream – shared, he said, by his wife, a doctor who could not join them today as she was working in the operating theatre of a nearby private hospital. Richard thought he said St Walburga's. Not a saint he'd ever heard of. He'd have to google it. Could be a talking point.

'You'll meet Hermione at some stage,' said Lincoln. 'But I'm the point man for these preliminary skirmishes.'

'You work from home?' Richard asked, as they walked into a smallish room Lincoln described as his office. A glass and chrome desk stood against one wall, devoid of any sign of activity, save a MacBook Air, closed. A small bookcase was full of neatly arranged DVDs. Framed advertisements lined the walls.

'Resting just now, in point of fact. I'm in the process of setting up on my own, but my previous employer's contract prevents me from doing anything competitive for a month or two. Here's my new card.'

Richard glanced at it. *Lincoln the Hunter*, it said, over a stylish coat of arms. There was an email address and a mobile phone number, and no other details.

'Marketing,' explained Lincoln. 'You'd know my work.'

'Oh?' Richard was intrigued. Perhaps there had been a huge payout, and that's where the money was coming from.

'You'll have seen the beautiful roses on *Bud*Jet aircraft?'

Richard dimly recalled a cut-price Asian airline that had attracted a brief flurry of publicity, but he had heard nothing more of it. He shook his head.

'The Ripper?'

Richard looked mystified.

'You're hardly the target audience, of course. Most success-ful snack-food product launch in living memory. I thought you might have seen the YouTube clip. Man in a black cape disrupt-ing some pollie's press conference? It was all over the news for a day or two. Does that ring a bell?'

'I do recall something on the news about a child who became seriously ill after eating a new –'

'Storm in a teacup. You'd know Cocky Cocktails, of course.'

'Of course,' said Richard, without conviction. 'Shall we look at the kitchen?'

As soon as Richard began to outline the concept of a convivium, the tone of the encounter changed radically. As if Richard had turned on a switch, Lincoln fell head over heels in love with the whole idea instantly.

'Awesome, Richard. That's simply awesome. No other word for it. I can already see it in my mind's eye.'

'A polished concrete floor, I think, Lincoln,' Richard went on. 'Travertine is a bit passé, don't you think? A bit of a cliché? Perhaps parquet . . . but, no, I think polished concrete. Lightly tinted, perhaps with Hermione's favourite colour. The merest hint, of course.'

Polished concrete? Parquet? Travertine? It was all the same to Lincoln. He was eager to welcome a convivium into his life, regardless of its flooring. But he saw larger possibilities as well.

'This is a game-changer, Richard, no question. *Convivium.* Wow! Have you registered the name? I assume we got it from the ancient Romans, right? If you ever decide to promote the idea with your own name firmly affixed to it, I believe I could be of some help. Definitely. Today an airline, tomorrow a convivium. Why not? I'm a gun for hire, just like you. When can we start work?'

'On a PR campaign?'

'Well, that too. No, I meant when can we get to work on the creation of our very own convivium, right here?'

Richard was simultaneously charmed and shocked by this un-bridled effusiveness. He'd never known a client to embrace any idea with such naked enthusiasm. It felt almost as if Lincoln were trying to sell *him* the idea.

While Lincoln kept staring at his kitchen/dining area, already transformed in his mind's eye, Richard was pondering two things. One was that the house barely felt lived in; it was too tidy; even the boys' room showed no sign of boys. The other was the structural difficulties involved in getting rid of two load-bearing walls, moving the bedchamber – Lincoln *loved* 'bedchamber' – from the front to the back of the house where it would overlook the bush, gutting and redesigning both bathrooms, and creating two small bedrooms for the boys where the original master bedroom had been. He did some pacing, ran the tape measure over a couple of rooms, took some photos and promised to email some concept sketches and a preliminary quote, 'a ballpark figure'.

As he was leaving, there was tentative talk of a second storey in a re-pitched roof with dormer windows. 'We might stick the boys upstairs, out of the way,' Lincoln said. 'Hermione says they'll be gone before you know it, although a former colleague of mine says this generation keeps coming back.'

Clearly, money was no object, after all.

They shook hands.

'Live the dream, bro,' said Lincoln.

The sight of his very own travertine-paved convivium gladdened Richard's heart, as it always did when he returned home, though he sensed the travertine's use-by date was fast approaching. Parquet was definitely having a revival. The dog might then become an issue, though. More of an issue. Perhaps polished concrete was the way to go.

'Home is the sailor, home from sea, and the hunter home from the Hunter.'

'What did you say?' Freya swivelled around in her chair. She no longer heard the words, but the disrupted rhythm of Richard's greeting was a surprise.

Richard plonked Lincoln's card on the table in front of Freya.

She picked it up, looked at it, turned it over. 'The hunter of *what*, precisely? Not big game, I hope.'

'No, he's some kind of marketing top gun, by the sound of it. Claims to have been the brains behind that airline that came and went. RamJet? Something like that?'

'Oh, *Bud*Jet? How could you forget? Worst flight Fern has ever had. She took one of the kids to Melbourne. It was bumpy – well, you can't blame the airline for the weather – and the service was non-existent. It seemed like quite an old plane. Cheap fare, of course. You get what you pay for. Anyway, to add insult to injury, when she got off the plane in Melbourne, she was handed a sad little rosebud that was clearly on its last legs, gasping for water. Never again, Fern said.'

'What about some kids' confectionery thing called the Ripper?'

Freya screwed up her nose. 'Oh, you remember that poor child who was poisoned by a snack-food product? I think that was called the Ripper. I'm pretty sure the child survived, but there was a dreadful stink about it. Isn't that an appalling name for a lolly! Is your hunter the brains behind that one, too?'

'Just the promotion, I gather. Not the product.'

'Gun for hire.'

'That's what he says. But that's me, too, of course. And Continental Drift. We're all guns for hire.'

'Well, some of us are gunnier than others, I guess.'

'Gunnier?'

'Have you eaten?'

'Yes – well, no, not really. By the way, he loved the idea of a convivium. Wants me to patent it or something. Practically knocked me over in his enthusiasm to get started. I think he almost loved the name better than the concept.'

'Great.'

Pause.

'He's keen on a polished concrete floor, too.'

Pause.

'Could we please not start on that again?'

'It's just that –'

'*Please*, Richard.'

'I'll go and change. How was your day?'

How *was* my day? Freya thought to herself, saying nothing, since Richard was already out of earshot. How *was* my day? When he comes back out here, I might just tell him.

She put some lasagne in the microwave and poured them both a drink.

Variatio 13. a 2 Clav.

13

Coming Home –
6th Variation – 'Reverse Angle'

Freya is sitting at the French farmhouse table. She hears Richard arriving home from work. His footsteps pause at the entrance to the convivium. *The convivium!* Why does she put up with this shit? She knows he is smiling. She knows how important it is to him that the travertine pavers, like the dog, came from Turkey. Oh, don't think we didn't consider sourcing them from fucking Guidonia Montecelio, but, no, Italian would have been 'boring'.

Wait, wait; he's going to say it. Don't say it, don't say it don'tsayitdon'tsayitdon't –

'Home is the sailor, home from sea, and the hunter home from the hill.'

One day, Freya thinks, I'll tell him that the line he endlessly quotes is from a poem about a cemetery. They're home, Richard, because they're dead. Home for all eternity. I don't wish you dead, Richard, of course I don't. I love you, you oaf. Why can't your words be as beautiful as your buildings? (I know, Mum. You can't have everything.)

She turns and smiles at him, hoping he didn't detect that little shiver. Not of revulsion, exactly. No, certainly not of revulsion. What, then? Just a little sign of . . . protest, resistance, weariness? Involuntary. Unkind. Unworthy.

'You okay, Frey?'

'I'm fine,' she says, and means to say: I really am fine. That shiver was nothing. I know there are things about me that drive you to distraction, too. Like my friendship with Daniel. Like what a lousy, reluctant cook I am. Like how I fail to moan like a porn star when we're making love. Like how seriously I take my work, when you think I'm merely in the entertainment game. The entertainment game! Well, yes. But, no, I'm fine.

How are you, my darling? How was your day? Why couldn't she bring herself to say things like that? Her mother could do it, year after year, for her father. No wonder he died with a smile on his face. She knew it would feel like a blessing to Richard. She'd say it tomorrow, for sure. No, not tomorrow – she had a late rehearsal. Soon, then.

'Have you eaten?' There. Isn't that a loving question? Even if reheated lasagne is all that's on offer. But he knows the rules – we take it in turns to cook, and we only bother if we haven't had a decent lunch. He'll have had an excellent lunch. 'Yes. Well, no, not really.' Why does he do that? Yes – well, no, not really. It's like when he can't think how to round off what he's saying to someone and there's an awkward pause and he says, 'So, yeah . . . no.' Is the world going to end tomorrow, Richard? 'Well, no one knows, do they, so yeah, no, not really.' It makes him sound like a fence-sitter, which he most assuredly is not. Nor an equivocator. Not Richard. Quite the reverse. So it's just a verbal tic, and a really, really irritating one.

'I suppose you ate at Beppi's.' It's not a question. Of course he ate at Beppi's. Does he love Beppi's? The question doesn't arise. He eats at Beppi's. Daily. Unless he's too far away to get there for lunch – like in Europe, for instance. He takes clients to Beppi's. He takes prospects to Beppi's. He sometimes takes colleagues to Beppi's. He eats alone at Beppi's. He takes Freya to Beppi's and expects her to act as if it's a special occasion even though he treats it like his staff canteen the rest of the time.

Freya waits for him to notice her skirt. Her little welcome-home treat. He notices it, strokes her shoulders, pulls her out of her chair, embraces her, runs his hands over her bottom, enjoying both the curves and the skirt. It is a beautiful skirt – quite sexy in its way – and very useful for distracting Richard, or softening him up, when that becomes necessary. Like when the Baby Question has to be raised. As it must be raised, with increasing urgency. For some couples – most couples – the Baby Question can be settled by natural means. We want to have a baby. I'll go off the pill. We'll make love as if we want a baby and, if we haven't left it too late, there will be a baby. It was that easy for Fern and Mike. But it was certainly not that easy for Daniel and Lizzie. And it will never be that easy for Freya and Richard.

So the skirt is both beautiful and useful. Just like me, thinks Freya ironically, seeing herself through Richard's eyes.

Freezing Richard's sperm won't be a problem. Finding an egg donor and a surrogate won't be a problem. Getting Richard to agree to freeze his sperm – to agree to the entire strategy – that will be the problem. And time is of the essence. Even if they are not going to use her eggs, it's her energy that is going to be needed to care for the baby. At thirty-nine, nature appears to have decreed that she's too old, and Mother Nature is worth listening to, surely. Freya doesn't want to be a figure of fun: a first-time mother in the body of a middle-aged woman. 'Oh, is that your grandson?' It would be a bit like those bizarre cosmetic surgery outcomes – the face of a forty-year-old perched on the neck of a sixty-year-old.

'No, you're busy,' Richard says. Amazing. He's acknowledged that working on a score counts as being busy. Progress. 'I'll get something. Can I get you anything?'

'No, I'm fine. I ate earlier.' Don't hide it. Don't hesitate. 'I had a late lunch with Daniel.' As we often do after rehearsals. So what? Richard is silly about this.

Is it really some weird jealousy of Daniel that stops Richard from asking how the rehearsal went? Or how Daniel's new baby is? Well – that's complicated. He wouldn't want the word 'baby' to pass his lips in case it worked like a trigger.

She lets him kiss her again, and it's warm and reassuring and . . . Richard is actually a great kisser. One of the things she admires about him.

She smiles and says, 'You go upstairs and change. I'll heat some lasagne and pour us a glass of something.'

She rattles around in the kitchen. Richard loves that sound, she knows. Must be connected to his troubled adolescent home life. Well, it's not hard to make a bit of noise with a few saucepans and plates, if it makes him feel securely loved. He is securely loved.

Now he's back in the convivium, they're raising their glasses and he's saying his crass 'Cheers'. Does he only do it to annoy her? To assert what they both know not to be true – that he's a regular Aussie bloke?

At least he doesn't begrudge her her practice time at home – at all hours of the day and night. And the studio is the Great Escape when Richard is eating and she isn't. You wouldn't call Richard a musical eater.

Safely locked away in her studio, Freya takes up her violin, tunes it and begins to play. Richard loves to hear her play. She loves to hear herself play. An inheritance from her father had allowed her to purchase a gorgeous Cremona fiddle that had taken her to a new level. One day, when she's rich and famous – ha! – Guarneri, Stradivari . . .

Richard is funny with compliments. He tells her she has a bottom like a peach, never acknowledging that she dislikes peaches, has always disliked peaches and has said, every time he buys peaches and offers her one, 'No, I don't like peaches.' So is her bottom furry? Slimy? Or just round? But most certainly not round like a peach. He used to compliment her on her hair until she pointed out the obvious problem – her hair, like her bottom, was a lucky genetic accident, barely distinguishable from Fern's hair, though very different from Felicity's lush red locks. (She and Fern think they know where that hair came from, but it's a topic they won't ever be raising with their mother.) Freya sometimes wonders whether she is too tough about such things. If Richard enjoys her hair – looking at it, stroking it, nuzzling it, smelling it – that's fine. But it's not an achievement to be praised. She'd much rather he praised her playing. And he does, though she always feels her concerts are more visual than aural for Richard. But he comes to all of them. That's nice. No – be fair, Freya. It's more than nice. He's devoted to you.

She runs over a difficult section of the score until it comes easily. That will have been long enough for Richard to have scraped his plate, belched, poured another glass of wine and scrolled through his texts and emails.

She emerges from the studio and they go through their dog-walking ritual. Once in a blue moon, Richard agrees to accompany her out of some misguided sense of duty towards her, rather than Rondo. 'We should spend more time together,' he sometimes says. 'We should talk more.' He reads stuff about relationships. It's that Socially Aware Architects mob. They have workshops about client relationships, and Richard comes home all fired up with the idea that they should work on their relationship. We're married, Richard, she says to him. It's fine. We're in the very thick of a relationship. We love each other – or, at least, we act as if we love each other, and what's the difference? We sleep in the same bed, clean our teeth in the same basin – though that's no longer true since he had the bathroom redone and installed twin wash basins. We make love as if we mean it – though not as frequently or perhaps as enthusiastically as we once did. We squint through heavy lids and grunt at each other over breakfast. We do practically everything together except our respective jobs. Please don't analyse our relationship, or goodness knows where we will end up. And don't come dog-walking on my account.

Freya had had to explain to Richard that, since he had insisted on choosing the breed of dog – a Turkish Kangal – it was only fair that she should insist on choosing the name. Rondo alla Turca. After a bit of prodding, Richard got it. But he never thought it was particularly clever. Or funny. Does Richard lack a sense of humour? It's a question Freya prefers not to ask herself.

Out the door, Rondo straining at the leash, the night air waiting to caress her face. Ah. The night air. Every house she passes contains a life. A tragedy. An ache. A loss. A disappointment. She's not maudlin about this. Just realistic. She loves slow movements, minor keys, in music and in life. But, yes, vivace has its place and, yes, there is love inside many of those houses, too. Contentment. Joy, maybe. Even bliss, occasionally. Each life, like each piece of music, has a beginning, a middle and an end. But Music itself goes on and on and on.

Ah. The night air.

14

Coming Home –
7th Variation – 'Am I Boring?'

The sight of the travertine-paved convivium gladdened Richard's heart, as it always did when he returned home, though he was beginning to warm to the idea of polished concrete. Freya was sitting with her back to him, and her shoulders appeared to be shaking, though whether she was laughing, shivering, coughing or sobbing it was impossible to tell.

'You okay, Frey?' Richard asked as he kissed the top of her head.

'I'm fine,' she said, and Richard was relieved to hear it.

'I wish I could say the same.'

'Tough day?' Freya was working on a score she had been rehearsing, but now put it aside.

Richard grunted and headed for the bedchamber to change. Rondo, sensing trouble, slipped outside.

When Richard re-emerged in T-shirt, jeans and loafers, Freya said: 'Have you eaten? There's some lasagne in the fridge. I can heat it up in a jiffy.'

'Yeah. Great. Thanks. I had lunch with Briggs – probably drank too much and ate too little.'

'Where did you go?'

'Oh, Beppi's. Where else?'

Freya found Richard's unwillingness to experiment with restaurants rather disconcerting. When he took her out for dinner at night, it was almost always Beppi's. And always the same table. She assumed it was the very table where he sat with his clients. Not very romantic, though it had been *very* romantic on their first date, when Beppi's was new to her and she'd had no idea it was so routine for him.

'Have you ever tried any of the other restaurants nearby? Sagra or Verde? You must walk right past Verde on your way to Beppi's.'

'Beppi's is comfortable. They know me. We run an account there. Does that sound boring?'

Well, of course, it did sound boring to Freya. Dead boring. Freya and Daniel – and occasionally Olivia – never ate at the same place twice. Article of faith. But 'yes' didn't seem like the right thing to say to a man just home, dog-tired, edgy, defensive. Tense. Coiled spring syndrome. Imagine saying 'yes' to a question like that.

'Not boring, but I suppose it does say something about you. Loyal, perhaps? Loyal *to a fault*, maybe? A creature of habit? That's probably true. A man of simple, straightforward tastes – except we know *that* isn't true. Single-minded? Yes, but that's more virtue than vice, I guess.'

Freya was enjoying this little game. Richard had stopped listening.

'You know,' he said, 'that uppity little bastard Noakes told me I was boring today. Came right out and said it.'

Philip Noakes was a junior partner, something of a wunderkind in the profession. In his mid-thirties, pale-faced, hollow-chested, blond, prematurely balding – the polar opposite of Richard's physical type. Hugely talented. Bold. Imaginative. Highly sensitive to issues of sustainability and cost. *And* cutting a swathe through the profession. Awards. Articles written about him. An adjunct professorship. Recently appointed a partner in Richard's firm though he was almost ten years younger than Richard had been when he was offered a partnership. And, Freya had been led to believe, something of a protégé of Richard's.

'Really? In front of anyone else?'

Richard looked at his wife, reminded yet again that he didn't quite grasp how her mind worked. *In front of anyone else?* Wasn't it bad enough to be abused to your face by a younger colleague?

'Just the two of us. We were out of the office, having coffee, talking over a concept drawing Philip is developing for part of the Briggs project. He might have been on something. Or hungover. But he's been showing signs of becoming more bolshie. It's a good thing, up to a point. That's why we made him a partner. Gutsy. Feisty. Out there. Clients love being around him. I sometimes wonder if they think he's so fucking *creative*, it might rub off on them. I don't know.'

'So how did it come up?'

'How do you mean?'

'Telling you that you were boring. There must have been some reason behind it, however misguided.'

There was a longish silence.

'I might have said he was being a pretentious prat.'

'Oh, Richard.'

'But it's true – he *is* a pretentious prat. Actually, a *boring*, pretentious prat.'

Freya had heard Richard use precisely those words on several occasions when he was complaining to her about Philip Noakes. But when Richard said 'boring' he often used it to express some more general displeasure. 'How boring,' he would say, when a flight was delayed, even though such disruptions were the opposite of boring, really.

'So calling you boring was retaliation?'

Freya found this easy enough to imagine – grown men calling each other names, half in jest, half in earnest. She'd seen Daniel and Jean-Pierre do it during tense moments in a rehearsal. She and Olivia had watched, fascinated, while Daniel called Jean-Pierre 'a psycho Frog' and Jean-Pierre, in an accent that charmed Freya (this being the only aspect of his style she found charming), called Daniel 'a fucking Aussie bastard', enunciating the words as if reading from a phrasebook. Daniel thought Jean-Pierre unacceptably, ostentatiously eccentric; Jean-Pierre thought Daniel a philistine at heart, a mere technician. Freya thought they each had a point.

Richard shrugged. 'I'm the senior figure.'

Freya refrained from chanting: *Mine's bigger than yours.* She settled for: 'This all sounds rather untoward, I must say. I'm tempted to say it sounds rather *boring*. I'm surprised you seem to have taken it to heart. I can't imagine Philip will lose any sleep over it.'

'I just said it. He *meant* it.'

'Surely not.'

'He might have had a point. I was trying to pull him back a bit on some of his design ideas for the Briggs job. He thought my suggestions would make the facade a bit boring. *Boring!*'

'The facade? The *facade*? Oh, Richard, he didn't call *you* boring at all, did he? He criticised a design suggestion. The very thing you're supposed to encourage at Urbanski. Frank and fearless – isn't that the spirit of your partnership? Play the ball, not the man – or that poor single solitary woman? I've heard you say it a hundred times. Attack the work for all you're worth. Don't attack its creator.' A pretty fine line, Freya had always thought.

Another pause. Richard's face was flushed.

'So, *am* I boring?' he asked his wife – a question no husband should ever ask his wife. Not after twelve years of marriage.

Freya was astonished. She had never heard her husband raise such a question. *Am I boring?* This was uncharted territory. Was Richard, of all people, suddenly plagued by self-doubt? Suddenly insecure? Anxious? It seemed inconceivable. Richard the warrior prince. *Her* warrior prince. Of course he was boring – or at least predictable – much of the time. Perhaps most of the time. But you could equally say 'reliable'.

'You know what G.K. Chesterton says.' Freya was treading cautiously. 'There's no such thing as an uninteresting subject, only an uninterested listener. It's the same thing, isn't it? Boring is in the eye of the beholder. A state of mind. *No one's* inherently boring, Richard. It's just that we are bored by some people. Even events aren't inherently boring – they might be tedious, but tedium is a very different thing from boredom. We have to deal with tedium, but Mum always taught us that boredom was practically a sin.'

'So, *am* I boring? To you?'

Freya's mother had not only taught her children that boredom was a sin, she had also taught them the virtue of kindness. Be kind, she would say, quoting some Scottish clergyman she admired; you never know what inner struggles people are contending with. Everyone lives with shadows. Everyone is at war with themselves. Everyone knows tragedy, or the fear of tragedy. Everyone is frightened of something. Everyone carries some level of heartache. Kindness is like a healing balm. Why not be kind, when there's so much healing to be done?

Kindness, yes. What about honesty, though? Why be honest about something like this, when a slight varnish would be less hurtful, Freya thought. Brutal honesty has its place, but not, surely, in the courtesies of everyday life nor in the peculiar vulnerabilities of intimate relationships.

Only one safe course.

'Don't be ridiculous. You are adorable, and adorable isn't remotely boring. But are you projecting, by any chance? Am *I* boring to *you?*'

'Don't change the subject.'

'You haven't touched your lasagne. I'll heat it up again. And I'll make some tea. You've probably had enough to drink for one day.'

Variatio 15. andante

Canone alla Quinta. a1 Clav.

Volti

15

Dinner with Daniel

'Time for a quick bite, Oli?'

'Sorry, gotta dash.'

After most rehearsals, Freya and Daniel had a meal together, or coffee, or occasionally a drink, depending on the time of day. Olivia sometimes joined them, but she usually had to race away to pick up one of her kids from somewhere. They never invited Jean-Pierre.

Daniel had been in love with Freya since their high school days. Freya had loved him too, back then, but used to say that it was more like a brother-and-sister thing, not a romance. She knew him too well.

Daniel never stopped being in love with Freya, right through their time at the conservatorium and beyond. For a short time, Freya felt such a rush of affection for her old friend, she imagined this might pass for love. They began sleeping together.

When Freya discovered she was pregnant at twenty-two, it was a rude awakening. She declared they were both too young to become parents, too young to make any sort of commitment to each other, too young to know what the hell was going on. Daniel's protests were dismissed. He might enjoy dreaming of a life together; she didn't entertain it for a moment.

She told no one except Daniel about the pregnancy and had it terminated as quickly as she could arrange it. Then she went back to being Daniel's closest friend.

Daniel was still in love with Freya when she fell wildly, if briefly, in love with a trumpeter called Dave. *The Freya and Dave Show* was very full-on while it lasted, even though Daniel thought she was being rash. She discounted Daniel's opinion, on the grounds that he was still in love with her. Both her sisters loved Dave. Fern loved his energy and his ability to drag Freya out of what he called her 'string-quartetishness'; Felicity, then seventeen and already showing a wild and rebellious streak, loved his recklessness. Her father, by then terminally ill, just wanted to see his second daughter happily settled in a relationship. He had no particular objection to Dave. Freya's mother, on the other hand, found Dave too brash and arrogant, and too often either drunk or stoned. She thought his effect on Freya was generally negative. She thought Freya was too gentle to resist him, too forgiving of his many gaucheries.

Freya was only fleetingly besotted with Dave; she had never swooned over him the way she later swooned over Richard Brooks. But she moved in with him soon after they met, and when Dave rather unexpectedly declared he wanted babies, she was quite prepared to go along with it. Why not? She was at that time drawn to the idea of motherhood, her own mother was dying for grand-children to fill the looming void of widowhood, and Fern was showing no inclination to reproduce. Two miscarriages followed in rapid succession, with high drama – medical and emotional – attending both. Dave, rather like Henry VIII, really did want an heir, and he soon found a more reliable foetus-carrier than Freya.

So Freya moved back home, traumatised but far from heart-broken. She had some inconclusive tests, but came to think of herself as a poor pregnancy risk, and was relieved when, in the early weeks of her romance with Richard, she learnt that he had absolutely no desire for another child. Her powerful desire to try again came much later.

Daniel lived through all this with Freya. Having taken her to the abortion clinic when she was pregnant the first time, he had devotedly sat with her and her older sister Fern in the hours and days after each of her miscarriages. Dave was on the road with his band both times.

Daniel was still in love with Freya when she married Richard, but he could see that this was a serious matter for her. She was determined to make a good marriage and to be a good wife. This time, Daniel kept his reservations to himself. He never wanted to lose Freya as a friend.

He met Lizzie at Freya and Richard's wedding. She had been invited at the last minute to accompany a cousin who was a friend-cum-client of Richard's. Daniel was feeling as if he had been thrown over by Freya in favour of Richard. Though he knew that did not accord with the facts, he clung to it as a narrative that helped account for his bleak sense of vulnerability. Lizzie, a few years older than Daniel, was also in an emotionally fragile state, having just ended a five-year relationship with a married man who, for four of those years, had talked of leaving his wife. She told Daniel the story on their way from the ceremony to the reception.

Scarcely knowing what they were doing, they left the wedding reception early, went for a long walk and ended up in Lizzie's bed. Neither of them claimed to be in love, then or later, yet they admired each other intensely, laughed at the same things, enjoyed the same movies, read the same novels. Lizzie was a kindergarten teacher who really loved the kids in her class. Her taste in music was unsophisticated, but she was an eager pupil when Daniel began to introduce her to the kind of music he played.

Daniel and Lizzie had never declared their undying love for each other: they had decided they were 'modern best friends, with sex'. Secretly, Daniel felt Freya would always be his best friend, with or without sex.

Lizzie and Freya hit it off when they met, and Daniel had mixed feelings about that. He was always glad of opportunities to see Freya, but felt uncomfortable with her in the presence of Lizzie. Lizzie, no fool, sensed all this.

Eventually, Lizzie announced that she wanted a baby. By then, she was in her late thirties, and nature was refusing to oblige. A protracted IVF program followed before Lizzie had a successful embryo transfer. Nine months later, baby Felix was born without complications. Daniel was smitten.

Freya was insanely jealous of Lizzie's good fortune, though not of Lizzie herself, and she enjoyed seeing Daniel take to fatherhood with such relish. She was surprised to find she was able to hold the baby without any conflicted feelings. This was Daniel's baby and she was happy for him and for Lizzie.

As they walked to the cafe they had chosen, Freya slipped her hand inside Daniel's arm. She knew he liked her to do this, and she felt it was harmless enough. Best friends, and all that. She also knew it was a gesture that fed Daniel's longing for her, and she did not care to dwell on that.

They both ordered pasta and a glass of red wine.

At a certain point in the conversation, Daniel looked deeply into Freya's eyes and said: 'It will never be any different. I will love you like this until the day I die.' Daniel regularly made declarations like this – had been making them for years – and

Freya both resisted and welcomed them. She would love Richard to do something like this, say something like this, make her heart skip a beat like it did when Daniel said these absurd, unrealistic things.

'You have Lizzie,' she replied, 'and now you have Felix. Nothing we do or say to each other must ever impinge on any of that.'

'You didn't mention Richard.'

'Don't be silly, Daniel. I love Richard. Richard is my husband. You know that. I wouldn't ever do or say anything to upset Richard. How many times do I have to tell you that?'

'That's crap, for a start. You've told me that Richard doesn't like you hanging out with me like this, yet you still do it.'

'And what about Lizzie? Wouldn't she rather you went straight home from rehearsals and helped her with Felix? Aren't you keen to get home and see them *both*?'

'Ah, Freya.'

Freya knew that tone of voice. That dreamy look. That tilt of the still-boyish head. The flop of that long, unruly hair. She knew Daniel in ways she would never know Richard. But that wasn't necessarily a bad thing. There was no mystery about Daniel. He was about to declare his love for her, yet again, and while she had no reason to doubt the sincerity and purity of his attachment to her, she found she actually enjoyed the realisation that she was sometimes *not* on the same wavelength as Richard. Life with Daniel would have been endlessly romantic, reckless, and utterly irresponsible. Nothing practical would ever have got done and even the chaos might have become tediously predictable, as well as irritating. But, in small doses and within safe limits, it was still lovely to know Daniel adored her.

'Do you know, Freya, that every note I play, I play for you? Do you *really* know it? Do you know that one of the things I love most about our performances is that when we're on the concert platform, I can look at you – gaze at you – more intensely than at any other time because you can't pull a face, like you just did. You have to play on, looking sublimely lovely, and just accept that the man sitting over there is making love to you with his cello.'

Daniel had said the same thing, or very nearly the same thing, a hundred times or more. More. And Freya never tired of hearing it.

16.

Variatio 16. a 1. Clav.

Ouverture

16

Coming Home –
8th Variation – 'A Text from
Jean-Pierre'

The sight of his convivium gladdens Richard's heart, as it always does when he comes home, the delight only slightly dulled by his growing conviction that a polished concrete floor would be a marked improvement on the travertine pavers. The natural next step. *A building is a living thing, subject to constant decay and needing constant renewal.* That's a line that goes down better with clients eager to renovate than it does with Freya.

Freya is sitting at the farmhouse table – that table had certainly not been a mistake, in spite of her resistance to the cost – with her back to him. Richard notices that her shoulders are shaking, though whether she is laughing, shivering, coughing or sobbing it is impossible to tell.

'Home is the –'

'Shut up, Richard.'

So she is shaking with anger.

'You okay, Frey?'

'I am not okay. I am as far from okay as it is possible to be.'

Richard's mind runs quickly over the events of last night. All clear, as far as he can recall. And today has been uneventful, until now. They'd had a brief phone conversation and an exchange of texts about their expected arrival times at home, and it was agreed they wouldn't need to bother with a proper dinner. A plate of cheese and crackers is already out on the table, together with a plastic tub of potato salad and another of coleslaw, both from the deli. It seems safe to proceed.

'What is it?'

'See for yourself.' Freya hands him her smartphone and he reads the text message on the screen: *I'm out. J-P*

Richard scans the screen for a sign of the author, but doesn't recognise the number of the sender.

'Who is J-P? And what is he or she out of?'

These are innocent questions but they provoke more rage from Freya. She howls like an animal, her face reddening.

'Fucking Jean-Pierre. Gone. Left. Quit. Just like that.'

'Jean-Pierre?'

'Our second violinist, Richard. You have met him on at least five occasions. Do you never pay attention to anything or anyone to do with my work?'

Richard is stung. That feels like an unfair remark. He would describe himself as broadly supportive of Continental Drift, if somewhat detached from the fine detail.

'You feel upset.' That is a line Richard has recently picked up from a speaker at one of the Socially Aware Architects workshops on resolving interpersonal conflict.

Freya gazes at him, open-mouthed with disbelief. 'Upset? Yes, you could say upset. You could also say suicidal, homicidal . . . no, not homicidal, *genocidal*. I want to kill *all* Frenchmen.'

'Is that entirely rational, Frey?'

'*Entirely* rational, Richard. Today is Wednesday. It's actually Wednesday *night*. We have a major, major gig on Saturday night. Big event. Big money. New work. That is three days away. Count them, Richard. One, Thursday. Two, Friday. Three, Saturday. Three days. And the fucking Frenchman has quit. Cold. And by *text*.'

'No warning?'

'Ha. It depends what you mean by warning. Tantrums every single rehearsal. Maybe that was a warning. Storming out of today's rehearsal because of some light-hearted remark Daniel made. But never an actual, specific threat to leave the group. No.'

'Let me think about this while I get changed. There must be a rational solution.'

'Oh, there's a rational solution, alright. Track down the traitorous Frog and ram his phone down his Gallic gullet. If you could murder someone by text, I'd do it.'

Richard retreats from the danger area.

If he comes back in here with one of his smart-arse so-called rational solutions, I'll kill him, too, thinks Freya. What I need now is for him to let me *wallow*. I need some *sympathy*. Process, Richard. Not the rush to a conclusion.

As he changes his clothes, Richard ponders the problem and sees only three possible solutions. He suspects Freya is too distressed to think straight, so he assumes – hopes – she'll be grateful for the input of a calmer mind.

'Let me pour you another drink,' he says when he returns to a still-fuming Freya.

Richard takes his time, as if to demonstrate the level of calm required. Freya is controlling her breathing, knowing – fearing – what is to come.

'Cheers!'

'*Salute.*' No exclamation mark.

'There are only three possible ways out of this.'

'Richard!'

'Let me finish, Frey. First, you cancel the gig. Loss of face. Loss of income.'

'Not an option at all, Richard. Can we not do this, please?'

'I assumed that would probably be the case. Second, you might not have thought of this. You could play as a trio. I don't know what's on the program, but it may well be the case that the second violin part – *second* violin, right? – wouldn't be missed. See what I mean?'

Freya has clenched both fists into tight balls of repressed rage. It is some time before she speaks. 'Oh, yes, brilliant. I see what you mean alright. The house would be fine with a few windows and walls missing. Who needs all those windows and walls? Eh? Sometimes you can be a total idiot, Richard. And I mean *total*.'

'I don't think that's a reasonable analogy at all, Frey. All I'm saying is that second violin is a secondary part – by definition – and that half the audience might not even notice if it was missing.'

Freya is slowly shaking her head as if she simply can't believe what she's hearing. There is no level at which she can respond. No way into this.

Richard is undaunted: 'But let's say you are right, just for the sake of argument. You need a fourth player. Alright, that brings me to the third and most obvious solution. I'm sure you're already working towards it with your colleagues.'

'What? Killing Jean-Pierre?'

'Come on, Frey. I'm trying to be serious. Finding a replacement for Jean-Pierre.'

'Just like that. Wednesday night, for Saturday's gig, with a new work included in the program, written for us and rehearsed for a month. Find a replacement!'

'How hard can it be? The world is full of eager young violinists, some of them brilliant sight-readers bursting with talent. You've often said so yourself. Too many people studying music. Too many good players. Most of them will never make it.'

'Richard. Stop. Leave this to us, please.'

'But I only meant that –'

'*Richard!*'

'Three days' rehearsal. That's plenty. Sure, it'll be intense. But a good player. An accomplished player. It's only a matter of reading the music, surely. How hard can that be?'

'Oh, any old builder will do. It's only a matter of reading the plans. How hard can that be?' Freya's voice is bitter, sarcastic and shrill. She is seeing, once more, a weird side of Richard that she usually finds endearing but now, in a moment of crisis bordering on panic, finds repugnant and mildly psychopathic.

Richard shrugs. 'Up to a point. Any qualified builder with a bit of experience. Runs on the board. Yes, any *good* builder could read the plans. He'd get by.'

'No site meetings. No interpretation. No role for an architect once the plans are drawn. Is that really how it is, you moron? You *fucking* moron!'

'I think this discussion is becoming unproductive, Frey. I fully acknowledge that music is different from architecture. Or building. I was only trying to help. Just trying to clarify the options. I'm sorry. It's just that I think –'

Freya doesn't wait to hear what he thinks. She is already on her way to the bathroom, possibly to vomit – her most common response to high anxiety.

Richard follows and, through the closed bathroom door, persists. His voice is still calm, his demeanour still dignified. 'I'd only add that it's possible to be too precious about all this. When our technical skill reaches a sufficiently high standard, we call it art – whether it's architecture or music. There's nothing mystical or supernatural about it. That's all I'm saying. Focus on the technical aspect.'

A faint moaning from within.

'Frey?'

'Go away.'

Variatio 17. a 2 Clav.

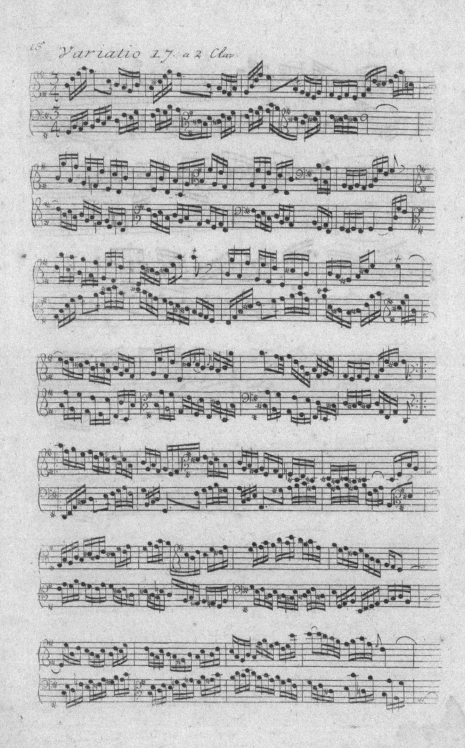

17

Schooldays

Russell, Geoff and Barry were at school together forty years ago and have kept in touch. They still meet three or four times a year.

'Hey! Did you see the little item in *Domain* about this brilliant architect who's come up with a new kitchen and dining concept – the convivium?' Russell fished a newspaper cutting out of his pocket. 'Guess who?'

Geoff grabbed the cutting and ran his eye over it. 'Richard Brooks! Is that our very own Richard Brooks?'

'Babble himself,' Russell said.

'It's not like him to be such a self-promoter.'

'I agree. That was my first thought when I saw the item. An image of Richard Brooks came back to me and I thought, this is very uncharacteristic of Babble. And as far as I can see it's just a fancy name for an expanded kitchen and dining area.'

'Yeah, Babble was never a bragger,' Barry said. 'The dead opposite, in fact. But the name. Convivium. That's pure Babble. Latin, is it?'

'Search *moi*.'

'We should look him up, you guys. We should never have lost touch. He was a wreck by the time we left school, even though he always shone in exams. I don't know. All that stuff with his father going off and then his mum dying. We never found out what his mother died of, either. Babble was always vaguely miserable, or something – except for that one time.'

'I was quite close to him at school. But I think I was a bit heartless, given what he must have been going through.'

'I always liked him too. I vaguely thought of looking him up. Someone told me he'd done architecture, so I thought he must be getting on alright.'

'Yeah. Well, he wouldn't be hard to find. Especially not now he's famous. Sort of. The name of his firm is here.'

'You said "except for that one time". What did you mean?'

'You remember – the poetry thing.'

'Remind me.'

'The end of year ten. After his life had fallen apart, more or less. Did you ever visit him at his grandmother's house?'

'Once. It was on a weekend. Yeah. I only went the once, though.'

'You're not Robinson Crusoe. I don't think anyone ever went back for a second dose of Grandma . . . what was her name? It wasn't Brooks. Can't remember. He always called her –'

'Grandma Davies. Something like that. She was ferocious. And the house had this terrible smell.'

'Arsenic and old lace.'

'Precisely. And the old crone was as deaf as a post.'

'Poor Babble. Why did he ask us to his house? Hardly anyone did that. Maybe he needed relief from the old woman. She always seemed to sort of hover over him.'

'But what was the poetry thing? I dimly remember Babble was nuts about poetry. Is that what you mean? He could memorise stuff like it was going out of style.'

'Poetry was his big thing. He wrote it, too, you know.'

'You're kidding.'

'No, really. He once showed me something he'd written. A long love poem to that girl – what was her name? The girl he took to the year ten formal? He was clearly crazy about her, but never even held her hand, according to Sarah, who always knew everything.'

'God. Sarah. I haven't thought about her in years. She's probably the mother of four brilliant children and running a merchant bank.'

'I think her name was Angie, the girl Babble took to the formal. That's it – short for Angelina. Pretty unusual name back then. She was a stunner. I could never work out how Babble convinced her to go with him. Didn't she get pregnant in year eleven and have to leave school?'

'Probably. I can't remember. Not many schoolgirls were on the pill in the seventies. I do remember that. Condoms or risk it.'

'Get to the point, Baz. The poetry.'

'Surely you remember the assembly where the headmaster announced that Richard Brooks was going to recite "Requiem", that Robert Louis Stevenson poem, in memory of his mother?'

'I do now. Of course! Bloody Babble. Talk about gutsy.'

'There was a lot of tittering and murmuring as he marched up to the dais. He wasn't exactly the most popular kid in the school, as we all know. Hopeless at sport. A lot of the guys thought he was pathetic, but he certainly wasn't pathetic. A bit aloof, maybe – that faraway look he often had. A strange bugger, to say the least. Anyway, I remember how he held his head up as he reached the dais, as if he was somewhere else.'

'God! I haven't heard that poem in years. I haven't heard *any* poetry in years. Ha! My wife sometimes says I need more poetry in my life. She might be right. What about you guys?'

'Poetry? No. Never. Not since school.'

'Go on about Babble. I do vaguely remember this. Got a big reaction, didn't it?'

'A big reaction? Are you kidding? Babble stood there beside the head until everyone was quiet. Then the head sat down and there was just Babble. Cool as a cuke. Launched into it like a professional actor or something.'

'Jesus, Bazza, you're bringing a lump to my throat. I *do* remember this. It was magical. The assembly hall had never been so quiet. I think a lot of the kids hadn't known about his mother's death and everything, so they didn't really get the significance of it until the head announced it. Or maybe not until Babble launched into it.'

'I remember how it started. We all had to learn it after that. *Under the wide and starry sky / Dig the grave and let me lie.* Good God, I *do* remember it.'

'Go on, then.'

'Not sure of the next bit . . . *Glad did I live* . . . something, something . . . *and gladly die*, of course. *And I laid me down with a will.* It was pretty grim stuff.'

'I forget how the second verse started, but I do remember the next line. *Here he lies where he long'd to be –*'

'Except Babble said, *Here* she *lies where* she *long'd to be.* I'm sure he did. I can even remember the head reacting when Babble said that. I'm rather glad you brought this up, Bazza. This is really strange. I can see Babble's face as if it was yesterday. Completely impassive.'

'Not a word you'd have thought of in year ten.'

'Quite. But I might have said dignified.'

'Yeah, Babble *was* sort of dignified, wasn't he? In spite of everything.'

'Maybe *because* of everything.'

'I've still got our class photo. I'm going to look it out.'

'Come on. Who remembers the last two lines?'

'Who could forget them? They haunted me for about six months after we learnt the poem in the Great Gaspy's English class. Christ, I haven't given the Great Gaspy a thought in forty years, either – I suppose he died of emphysema aeons ago. Anyway, the ending. *Home is the sailor, home from sea –* '

All three joined in the final line: '*And the hunter home from the hill.*'

'Yeah,' said Russell. 'Old Babble, eh? What a performance.'

They fell silent.

'You remember how it ended?'

'Vividly, now you've taken me back. He turned to the head and sort of half bowed. Then he stepped off the dais and walked back to his seat. Same thing – head high. Not a peep out of anyone. I think some kids were actually choking up.'

'Then the eruption. Remember? Huge. Tumultuous applause. They clapped and clapped. It was like a sympathy vote. The biggest moment of Babble's school career. No question.'

'Richard Brooks the architect. Bugger me. Good old Babble.'

'We should get in touch.'

'Yeah, we really should.'

18

Coming Home –
9th Variation – 'A Meditation'

The sight of his travertine-paved convivium gladdened Richard's heart, as it always did when he came home, but tonight the thrill was fleeting. It was now clear to him that the space would be immeasurably improved if they were to rip up the tiles and replace them with . . . what? Travertine had definitely become a cliché, gone the way of plantation shutters. Parquet was having a revival but might already be passé. Polished concrete was probably the answer. The fad had passed, but there was a timeless quality about polished concrete that appealed to Richard. Untinted, of course. It could even look original.

He almost spoke, but then remembered.

Freya was usually home before him, and he was always disappointed when she wasn't. Tonight, her empty chair seemed particularly eloquent. A little surge of disappointment, tinged with anxiety, flowed through him.

He knew where she was. He knew it could be a very long night.

Rondo, asleep on the floor of the convivium, raised his head to acknowledge Richard's arrival. This was not the person Rondo really wanted to see, but he dragged himself to his feet, trotted over to Richard and allowed himself to be patted. On Fridays, he was walked and fed by the son of a neighbour, so there was nothing Richard could offer him beyond a pat. In return, Rondo nuzzled Richard's crotch. Having thus exchanged tributes, Rondo returned to his corner, dropped to the floor and was instantly asleep again.

Richard stood for a moment inside the doorway. Then he said out loud, to the empty room, those lines that never failed to steady him: 'Home is the sailor, home from sea, and the hunter home from the hill.' How could the recitation of something so sad, so poignant, be so therapeutic? He knew the answer to that, of course. So why had he never explained it to Freya? Why was it so hard to reveal certain things to her – intimate things, significant things, deeply personal things? He wasn't even confident of his ability to convey to her the true significance of the project he was trying to persuade Briggs to support – its *emotional* significance for him. Once or twice, when a project dear to his heart had failed to materialise, Freya had said, 'It's only bricks and mortar, after all.' He assumed she meant it as a comfort, but it had felt like a body blow to him.

There had been a breakthrough over lunch in his negotiations with Briggs. It was starting to look as if Madrigo, their low-cost housing project, might finally become a reality. It was the thing he wanted to do more than anything else in the world. More than the extravagant renovation for Lincoln the Hunter and his still-invisible wife, Hermione the Doctor. More than yet another commercial high-rise, no matter how grand or how pretty. More than any concrete-and-glass bunker perched on some expensive hillside overlooking the crystal sea. Richard had always believed it was possible to put real style and real quality – real *beauty* – into low-cost housing, including public housing. He wanted Madrigo to be recognised as an example of medium-density housing design at its best, regardless of cost. That was the whole point. He wanted the occupiers – renters and owners, but especially renters – to be proud of where they lived. He wanted them to get an aesthetic kick out of coming home.

Once, when he was buying a car, the salesman had said that considering this was the second-biggest purchase most people made, you should only buy a car that gave you pleasure every time you sat in it. That was exactly the feeling Richard had always wanted to create for people who lived in low-cost housing. Too many people were trapped in those infamous little boxes. No charm. No style. No soul. It was all a matter of design.

It was also a matter of finding a developer who agreed with him and now, finally, he had found Briggs. It would be slightly less of a financial killing than Briggs was used to making, but he would still make a handsome return, and Richard had promised him that he would be rewarded in other ways. The gratitude of residents. His name on a plaque at the front of the building. (Briggs, who never smiled, smiled at that.) When it had sounded as if Briggs was going to insist on all the old familiar compromises, Richard had briefly thought of bringing Lincoln the Hunter in as a kind of advocate. But now it looked as if he was on the brink of pulling it off on his own.

He was exultant. Elation was not something Richard was accustomed to feeling, but he was deeply, deeply certain that if this project went ahead, it would cement his reputation, perhaps even internationally.

Beauty and utility. Take utility to the highest possible standard of refinement and it becomes beauty. He believed that.

Madrigo might well turn out to be the biggest coup of his professional life, but all he wanted now – *all* he wanted – was to be able to tell Frey; to share it with Frey; to see the pleasure he hoped Frey might take in his achievement, once she understood the unique character of this concept.

She might not be home for hours.

Throughout the twelve years of their marriage, the richest moments of his working life were the ones he shared with her. *And she probably did not know that.* Every one of his professional attainments only became a vivid reality for him once Freya had responded to it. *And she probably did not know that.* He knew the reverse was not true: he knew the satisfactions of her musical life existed independently of his response to it, and he thought he understood why. But, since marrying Freya, his own professional life finally made sense to him only through her reactions. Was that dangerous? Was he dependent on her to an unhealthy degree? Possibly. Too bad. That's how it was. Frey was his muse, his confidante, his one-woman cheer squad, his comforter. The only woman he had ever completely trusted. He *was* dependent on her. That was the truth. And he experienced it as a beautiful truth.

Yet here was the strangest thing: he seemed quite unable to say any of that to her. He had tried once or twice, haltingly, but it came out sounding stiff and contrived. He sometimes – often – fantasised about sitting at the farmhouse table opposite Frey, taking both her hands in his, looking directly into her eyes and *telling* her what she meant to him. But it had never happened.

Couldn't do it. Too awkward. Too embarrassing. Couldn't find the words.

He put it in writing, as best he could, in birthday cards. But he was not a wordsmith. He was an architect. He thought of himself and his colleagues as artists. And artists, he knew, were notoriously poor spellers – perhaps that was a symptom of their lack of facility with language. That kind of language.

His buildings were his messages to the world, and they were his messages to Freya, too. And, increasingly, he saw that his work was his *response* to Freya. He knew she didn't realise that. (How could she if he never said?)

Actions speak louder than words. Handsome is as handsome does. Was that meant as some kind of consolation, Freya saying those things? Or was there a wistful edge to these various aphorisms she recited? More than one woman in his life had insisted you had to put these things into words. On the day she deposited him at Grandma Davis's house, his mother told him that his father had never once said that he loved her. As if that had been the most heinous of his crimes.

Richard climbed the stairs to the bedchamber, changed into his jeans and a T-shirt, and saw Freya's long black skirt thrown over the back of a chair. He was irrationally pleased she hadn't worn it to her rehearsal. He picked it up and buried his face in it. There was another way of putting all this: he was addicted to Freya. Cheerfully so, with his eyes wide open.

Downstairs, he poured himself a drink, then poured it back into the bottle and boiled some water for tea. The note on the fridge said there was lasagne (of course) to heat up if he needed something to eat. He didn't. Lunch with Briggs had gone until almost five. Then there had been Friday drinks and a pizza with his colleagues. General – if somewhat premature – rejoicing over the Briggs job. Still no signature on the contract, but he knew they were already thinking about the fees. None of them, he felt sure, appreciated the scale of the contribution this project would make to Richard's view of himself as a radical architect.

Now he needed Freya to know. He would try to explain the real meaning of this project to her, to excite her, but she would be tired – exhausted – and stressed from trying to fill Jean-Pierre's shoes at short notice. Would he be able to restrain himself and say nothing about Briggs until the morning? Probably not.

He wandered into her studio, her perfume faintly in the air. This was her factory, he thought. This was where she really earned her living – in the endless hours of sweat and toil. Talent? Everyone said how talented she was. How gifted. But he had never known anyone to work as hard as Freya at honing her talent into something so extraordinary it looked effortless. He never spoke of this. Never gave her credit for what she put into her musical life; not in words, at any rate. It was tricky. If he expressed his wonderment at the amount of work she put in, it might sound as if he wasn't properly acknowledging her talent. If he praised her talent, it might sound as if he was downplaying the effort or implying she got by on talent alone – a bit like her beautiful hair that was 'only genetic'.

Why could he never find a way to say all this?

He always complimented her after a performance, and meant every word of it, though he often wondered if his compliments seemed shallow to her. He was quickly out of his depth when she analysed the finer points of a piece with her colleagues, or when she was fielding compliments from people who obviously knew what they were talking about. And let's be honest, Richard sometimes said to himself, a lot of the new stuff they played was pretty borderline. Was it really music at all? He had tried to discuss this with Freya but she quickly grew defensive. She told him that any sound extended was a musical note. *Any* sound. And she said that music was about evoking an emotional response. *Any* response. Fair enough. Sometimes this stuff made him feel edgy, almost angry, and Freya seemed cool with that. But she didn't seem so comfortable with the idea that staunch resistance, a tendency to mock, a squirming wish to get out of there, or a frustrated desire to hear something you could whistle also counted as legitimate emotional responses.

The thing he clung to was that these performances were as much about seeing the beauty of Freya on stage as about the music. The grace of her movements. The way she leant forward or back, or tilted her head. The vigour of it. The sheer fluidity of it. Beauty and utility – when they were both of such a high order, you couldn't separate them.

Only once, very early in their relationship, did he admit to Freya that he got a thrill out of thinking of her in bed with him while watching her perform on stage. She was displeased. Back then, she used to say that, for Richard, everything was about sex. And, back then, he conceded, everything *was* pretty much about sex.

Twelve years on? He desired her as much as ever, but of course it was different. Deeper. Less urgent. Sometimes troubled. But better. Definitely better.

He accepted that he would never be 'musical', in her terms. He would never be really comfortable in her world. But he really admired what she did and how she did it, and he hoped that was enough.

He looked around the studio. He could improve this space, he thought, with a minor bit of reconfiguration. Make it more beautiful, more compatible with what went on in here. The carpet was actually quite tacky, now you looked at it. Perhaps, post-travertine, some of the convivium pavers could be salvaged and re-laid here, with that rug Freya was always wanting him to find. He would raise that with her, and he would acknowledge that acoustics would of course be a factor in how they redesigned the space. But, mainly, he would try to express how he felt about her work. He knew that, if you totted it up, you would find he talked far more about his work than about hers. And he probably didn't listen as attentively as he should, but that was partly because he couldn't appreciate music the way serious musicians did. (Non-architects, including Freya, had the same problem appreciating the nuances of his own work. He had learnt to live with that.)

That business with the French second violinist. That was outrageous. But once something like that had happened, all you could do was work around it. Richard realised, in retrospect, that Freya hadn't wanted his advice at all. All she had wanted was sympathy – and he did feel sympathetic, but also, he had to admit, a bit impatient at her reluctance to find a solution and move on. He acknowledged, too late (always too late), that she and her colleagues were perfectly capable of dealing with the problem. The fill-in woman they'd managed to find sounded a bit of a handful, but what did he know?

It was funny, Richard reflected, that it was so hard to say the deep things you really wanted to say – the things Freya probably wanted to hear – and so easy to say all the stuff she didn't want to hear, like how he might go about solving her problems. Crazy.

The house was unnervingly silent. Richard briefly contemplated turning on the television before rejecting the idea and heading for his study.

His inbox contained a strangely guarded message from Briggs asking for another meeting next week – not cold feet, surely? It was all about selling, Richard reflected, not for the first time; it was all about closing the deal. The brightest ideas in the world soon lost their lustre without a backer. Even a poet needed a publisher. He had once quoted on a home renovation for an IBM executive who had a framed sign hanging in his office: *Nothing happens until someone sells something.* He had never quoted that to Freya, though it was as true for professional musicians as for architects.

He shut the computer, checked his phone in the vain hope of finding a message from Freya and went upstairs.

Are marriages always as unequal as this? he wondered. I am the luckiest person in the world when it comes to marriage, but who would say that of Freya?

She made him complete, but he knew he didn't make her complete. Not even music did that. She wanted a baby, on top of everything else.

He kicked off his shoes, threw himself on the bed fully clothed, and waited.

19

A Twilight Harbour Cruise

The sun was still high and bright in the western sky. Sydney Harbour was sparkling. A large and sleek white cruiser was tied up alongside a wharf in Rushcutters Bay, waiting for the forty-odd staff of Urbanski, with their spouses or partners and a handful of clients, to embark on a Friday twilight cruise.

This was the idea of Urbanski's senior partner, Paolo Sartori, the only member of the firm who had actually worked with Stefan Urbanski, the firm's founder, and who therefore felt he had some kind of apostolic link to the great man. He had decreed that all staff should attend, with partners. He had personally selected the charter boat, which he insisted, in his Mediterranean way, on calling a yacht, confusing his Australian colleagues for whom 'yacht' connoted masts and sails.

Freya was not the only spouse to have been a reluctant starter. Most spouses and partners had voiced their opposition to this expedition, mainly based on their resistance to the idea of being stranded on a boat for four or five hours, bobbing around the harbour with people they might have met once or twice at the firm's Christmas parties, but with whom they had nothing whatever in common, except, perhaps, the experience of living with an architect.

Freya's reluctance ran deeper than that. Though she had been a champion swimmer at school and still trained regularly, though she held a bronze medallion in surf lifesaving, though she loved the water, she simply hated boats. Even a mild chop was enough to induce nausea and she feared that if the weather turned at all rough, she would embarrass Richard by throwing up.

'It's just your anxiety,' Richard assured her. 'It's not true seasickness.'

'That makes no difference to the look or the smell of the vomit, Richard. Or to the depth of my humiliation. Why can't you all go off and have a jolly bonding experience on your own?'

'Try telling that to Sartori. Anyway, Briggs will be there, and I really want him to meet you. Madrigo is very close to being a done deal and, well, I just think it would help if you could spend a bit of time with him. That's all. It will be a very casual setting, obviously.'

'Do you know how awful that sounds, Richard? Am I to be some kind of bait, dangled in front of the wretched Briggs? How is this going to affect the question of whether your plans for Madrigo make sense to him or not? He's a businessman, Richard. A developer. It'll all come down to the bottom line. You've said so yourself. Many times.'

'I didn't put it very well. I'm sorry, Frey. All I meant was that I would like Briggs to feel as if he knows another side of me. Warm him up a bit.'

'Warm him up a bit? Did I hear you say *warm him up a bit*?'

'All I meant –'

'I know what you meant, Richard. I just enjoy watching you squirm. I'll charm the pants off your Mr Briggs. He won't know what hit him.'

And so here she was with Richard's colleagues and the other spouses-or-partners, milling around like kids on a school excursion, jostling to get on board quickly enough to secure a prized upper-deck spot. Up until the last moment, Freya had been hoping that something would go wrong, that some disaster would intervene to prevent the whole thing going ahead. The weather would turn so foul they would have to call it off; Paolo

Sartori would be rushed to hospital – nothing serious – and they would all go home out of respect for him; the boat would magically sink to the bottom, right there at the wharf, before anyone had boarded it; there would be a bomb scare. Anything.

Nothing.

They were all boarding like lambs. So Freya lined up, smiled wanly at Richard, and joined the general surge.

It began surprisingly well. Never one to stint, Paolo Sartori had selected a vessel so luxurious that the passengers were immediately seduced by it. Sartori himself came over the PA system, welcoming everyone on board like a tour guide, and announcing that the bar was now open and food would be served when they reached Camp Cove.

The drinks flowed freely. Lulled by the gentle movement of the boat and the hum of its twin diesels, the mood soon became mellow. Staying close to shore, they glided around Darling Point and Double Bay, then cruised on past Point Piper and into Rose Bay, many of the passengers casting a professional eye over the waterfront real estate they were passing, some of it the work of Urbanski. Finally, they rounded the point into Camp Cove, where a crew member in a nautical blazer, pale slacks and stylish leather gloves produced a length of rope so clean and white it looked like a design accessory and secured them to a buoy. Food began to appear. It was plentiful and delicious and, now that the boat had stopped, even Freya was beginning to enjoy herself. Seated outside in the fresh air, on the lower deck near the stern, she'd temporarily lost sight of Richard and had not yet been introduced to the infamous Briggs.

There came a sudden shout from above and, a split second later, Freya caught a peripheral glimpse of a fully clothed body falling from the upper deck on the other side of the boat. A loud splash was followed by the unmistakable sounds of waterlogged panic.

Rushing to the rail, Freya saw a figure thrashing helplessly in the water, gurgling, spluttering, and dipping below the surface, already being carried away from the boat by the strong current of an ebb tide. Without a pause, Freya tore off her jeans, kicked off her sandals, clambered over the rail and executed a perfect dive, coming up close to the increasingly desperate flounderer.

'Just relax,' Freya said, as she grasped the forlorn figure in her lifesaver's grip. 'It's okay. I know what I'm doing. What's your name?'

'Philip,' he coughed. 'Philip Noakes.' Then he moaned softly and brought up a copious combination of seawater and seafood. He had clearly dined well, if a little too hastily.

'I'm Freya,' she said, dragging him away from the contaminated area and, in the process, drifting still further from the boat. The tidal pull was stronger than she had expected in such a protected bay. 'I'm Richard's wife. You'll be okay, Philip. Just try to stay calm. Focus on your breathing – count three in and three out. Have you had much to drink?'

'Too much. Far too much,' said Philip, bringing up a little more of the noxious marinade.

She turned him on his back and began working her way towards the boat, talking quietly to him the whole time, even remembering to congratulate him on his recent appointment as a partner in the firm.

'A rope, please – *now!*' she called, as she trod water with Philip still securely in her grasp and lying quite still, his humiliation having driven out all traces of panic. The watchers crowding the upper and lower railings were stunned into silence by Freya's aplomb.

'Jesus. Who is *she*?' asked Briggs.

'My wife,' said Richard, his voice hoarse from a combination of pride and shock.

A rope was finally produced – why a lifebuoy had not been despatched in the first place was the focus of a subsequent inquiry into the incident – and thrown to Freya, who looped it expertly under Philip's arms and knotted it across his chest. Then she guided him to the side of the boat where a few strong hands hauled him out of the water and onto the deck. He lay breathless and sodden, like a half-drowned puppy – or, as Richard thought less charitably, like a legless drunk caught in a downpour.

'He's lost one of his shoes!' exclaimed Noakes's wife, so overcome by embarrassment that she seized on the lost shoe as if it were the most significant thing to have emerged from all this.

'He's lost one of his shoes,' someone relayed to Freya, who was still treading water beside the boat.

'I'll see if I can find it,' she said, launching herself into a duck-dive and disappearing beneath the waves. There was still plenty of daylight, and the water was reasonably clear and quite shallow where the boat was moored. After three attempts, Freya surfaced with the missing shoe held aloft like a trophy. A few people clapped and cheered uncertainly, wondering if they should have done more to help.

Philip Noakes, meanwhile, was bundled into the cabin, where his wife removed his sodden clothing and wrapped him in towels. His teeth were chattering and he was still expelling little bubbles of water like a baby oozing milk after a feed.

Back on the rear deck, Richard had retrieved Freya's clothes from where she had abandoned them, and was throwing her a rope. She looped and knotted it around herself, and allowed Richard, supported by the goggle-eyed Briggs, to haul her up to the deck. A crew member, resplendent in his blazer and still clutching a platter of biscuits and cheese, watched with keen interest. He would say later that he had kept a close eye on everything, but that the passengers, especially Mrs Brooks, seemed to have it all under control.

Once Freya was safely back on board, Richard, with Briggs hovering, rubbed her down with a towel and helped her back into her clothes.

'We should obviously get Philip onto dry land and back home asap. I'd like to go with him,' Freya said, 'just to keep an eye on him. At least he didn't hit his head on the way down.'

Richard, overwhelmed by Freya's display of courage and skill, was ready to agree to anything. He went and had a word with Philip and his wife, who acknowledged that getting Philip off the boat and into a hot shower were their top priorities. They lived in nearby Dover Heights, they told him, only minutes away.

Richard called a cab on his mobile; a pair of dry, if ill-fitting, tracksuit pants were located for Philip; the captain eased his craft alongside the jetty, and they were in the cab and on their way home within fifteen minutes of Philip being fished out of the water. Paolo Sartori had stood at the gangway as they disembarked, bowing extravagantly, kissing Freya's hand and expressing undying gratitude and admiration for what she had done. He restrained himself from scowling at Philip.

Though Richard made a half-hearted offer to accompany her, Freya insisted he stay and schmooze Briggs.

Once it had become clear that no serious damage had been done, except to Philip Noakes's pride, the party mood on the boat took hold once more. It was enlivened by the unspoken thought shared by most of Philip's colleagues that, if such a thing had had to happen to someone, they were quite pleased it had happened to him.

20

Coming Home –
10th Variation – 'Busy, Busy'

The sight of his convivium gladdens Richard's heart, as it always does when he comes home. Freya is sitting at the farmhouse table with her back to him. Her shoulders are shaking, though whether she is laughing, shivering, coughing or sobbing it is impossible to tell.

'Home is the sailor, home from sea, and the hunter home from the hill,' says Richard, hoping that, if Freya is upset, the familiarity of these lines might reassure her. Cheer her. Calm her.

Her shoulders continue to shake and she fails even to acknowledge that Richard is there or that he has spoken.

He moves to stand behind her, placing a hand on each shoulder and kissing the top of her head.

'You okay, Frey?'

The shaking resolves itself into a shudder. She has still not looked at him. A half-empty bottle of white wine stands on the table, with just one glass (freshly refilled, Richard notes with a tinge of anxiety).

When she finally turns her gaze on him, he is shocked by the look on her face. If it were not his wife, if it were not Freya, he'd have said it was a look of hatred. But he can only interpret it as distress. When she speaks, her voice is trembling. 'Have you any idea what time it is?'

Richard instinctively looks at his watch, though he knows it is roughly the same time he gets home most nights. Why would Freya be drawing his attention to such a normal event?

'A bit after eight,' he says cautiously, but with a touch of defiance he hadn't intended to convey.

'A bit after eight,' Freya parrots. There is a mocking edge

to her voice that Richard finds unnerving. Freya appears to be very angry.

'Is something wrong, Frey? Is there something you're not telling me? Have I forgotten something that's on tonight? Are we supposed to be going out?'

'Out? *Us?* Ha. Something on tonight? What would be on tonight, Richard? When is anything ever "on"? Yes, it's a bit after eight o'clock, Richard. Quite a bit, in fact. It's almost nine.'

'And?'

'You'll be gone again by seven-thirty, I assume. Eleven hours at home, and most of them sleeping. Ten or eleven hours at home and thirteen or fourteen hours away from home. Day after day after day. Such a busy, busy little bee.'

'Yes, it is a busy time.'

'A busy *time?* What, the last five years?'

'It's not always so busy. But, yes, this is a busy patch.'

'Maybe you're slowing down, Richard. Maybe you're getting old. Maybe you're just less efficient than you used to be. Less competent. Gosh! Maybe it takes you longer to do everything these days. Or maybe you spend too long over lunch at Beppi's, day after fucking day, with assorted cronies and conmen. God, what a world you live in, Richard. What a sleazy, grubby, grovelling fucking world. The client is king! The client is king! I've even heard you say it. You say it's about design. It's really about money.'

'Frey, I think –'

'Don't you dare put your patronising fucking hand on my shoulder, Richard. I'm just the wife. Filling in the endless hours when you're not here. Amusing myself with my little string quartet to keep me occupied during the long hours when the Great Architect is out changing the world.'

'Frey! That is ridiculous and you know it. I don't know anyone who's busier than you are. The quartet is a full-time job. Clearly. And the endless hours you put into practising . . . well, I'm really impressed. Perhaps I don't tell you that often enough. But it is a huge load. A huge load. I fully acknowledge that.'

'What the hell are you trying to say, Richard. That *I'm* busy?'

'Of course you're busy. Look at you now. You have a score and an iPad *and* your mobile in front of you. You were working when I came in. You're *always* working when I come in. In a minute, you'll offer me some reheated food for dinner and then you'll retreat to your studio and put in another hour or so of practice. I assume you do that at night because you're too busy to do it during the day. How would I know what you do all day?' Richard paused. 'Daniel seems to be a fairly major presence in your days, if I may say so, including lunches *and* dinners.'

Freya glares at him, too furious for speech.

'Look, Frey, I don't begrudge you any time you need to spend at your work. Have I ever complained? Do I complain when you have an evening gig? I come when I can but, if I have something else on, I don't complain when you get home at midnight or later. Or when you have to tour. We've both understood all this right from the beginning. Why is this suddenly an issue now?'

'Richard, do you know how you greet people on the phone, or even socially? Have you heard yourself?'

'I say hello, like everybody else.'

'No you don't. You say, "How are you – *busy*?", as if busyness is a fucking virtue. That's what you say. And I hear you on the fucking telephone endlessly telling people how busy *you* are.'

'How busy *we* are, Frey. We are *both* busy. When people ask me how we are, that's a natural thing to say. What else would I say? "Oh, we're both at a bit of a loose end. Not much on." Come on, Frey. What is all this?'

'Do you think people really want to know how busy you are? Do you, Richard? Do you think they're *interested*? Do you ever consider the possibility that they might actually be more interested in what you've been reading, or thinking about, or where you've been going and what you've been doing when you're *not* working?'

'Well, I –'

'Do you know what it reminds me of, Richard? It reminds me of old people who only want to tell you how well or how badly they've slept, or whether they've opened their bowels in the last twenty-four hours. *That's* what it's like. Boring, boring, boring. Oh we're so *busy*, everyone! Hey, want to hear how busy we are?'

'Give it a rest, Frey. This is just becoming silly. You can't deny that you are at least as busy as I am. You spend more time on your computer at night than I do. I basically come home and switch off.'

Freya springs from her chair and stands to face Richard, toe to toe.

'Switch off? *Switch off?* You spend at least as long as I do on your computer at night. When was the last time you came to bed without checking your emails? You're *addicted* to bloody email, Richard.'

Richard shrugs. 'I'm not going to count up the hours. All I can say is that my impression is that you're going non-stop. Maybe that's how it is for musicians. I don't know. My *impression* is that your days are very full.'

'Oh, yes, I can fill in my days as well as anyone. I'm talking about our nights. What used to be our nights *together*. Movies. Concerts. Plays. Dinner with friends. Short breaks away. Remember all that? Now it's the odd Saturday night if we're lucky or an occasional Sunday lunch with someone, usually with a business agenda attached or implied. *Fuck* you, Richard. You have disappeared. I never see you. You are exactly like my father was. You are so *busy*, so *preoccupied*, your head is no longer accessible to me. I have no idea who you are or what the hell you're thinking. Who *are* you, Richard? Richard Brooks the famous architect? Is that all there is? Where is Richard the man? Tell me that. Where has my husband disappeared to?'

Tears begin coursing down Freya's cheeks but she brushes them away and sniffs loudly.

There is a long pause, both of them breathing hard. Freya slumps back into her chair, elbows on the table, chin resting in her hands.

'I'll tell you one *busy* thing I did today. I spent an hour with Dr Costa at the fertility clinic.'

'Frey –'

'Don't panic. It's all doable. That's all I'm saying.'

'Frey, be serious. Look at yourself. Look at your life. Flat out with Continental Drift. Practising for hours on end. All the admin. All the marketing – I don't know what your agent does, to be frank. Do you honestly imagine there's room for a baby in your hectic schedule? Your schedule *is* hectic. At least, that's how it looks to me.'

'Oli manages perfectly well with two kids.'

'With respect, Olivia doesn't run the show. She does what you tell her.'

'Anyway, my mother has already agreed to step in when needed. That's what she did for Fern when her two were little. It would be even easier for her now Dad has gone.'

'So you'd happily cut back on the music? You'd give yourself over to motherhood? And you'd be satisfied with an only child – something you always said you'd never want to inflict on any child of yours?'

Richard is quite relieved, in a way, that they are back on the solid ground of rational argument. He'd have preferred a different topic, but at least the rant about busyness has subsided.

Freya is staring at him again. Glaring at him.

'Richard, listen to yourself. Do *I* imagine there's room for a baby in *my* schedule? *I'd* have to give myself over to motherhood. *I'd* cut back on the music. What about *you*, Richard? Parenthood is not just about mothers. Fathers are right in there, right in the thick of it. At least they are if they know what's good for them *and* for the child *and* for the marriage.'

'But I thought –'

'I know what you're going to say, Richard, so think again. I've been doing a lot of rethinking myself, amid all this busyness that's supposed to be crushing me. Whether I get pregnant naturally or we decide to do it via surrogacy, we'll have to be partners in this. No coming home at eight-thirty at night.'

'So is that what this –'

'No it isn't, as a matter of fact. I am sick to death of being married to a busy, busy, busy man. A man who seems to think it's good to be out-of-control busy. Sick of it. Baby or no baby. I want our life back, Richard. I want my life *with you* back. I want to feel as if we love each other again.'

'But of course we –'

Freya silences him with an outstretched hand.

21

A Misalliance

Had Richard known that this particular duo was meeting, hidden away like a pair of conspirators in a coffee shop not fifty metres from the offices of Urbanski, his antennae would have been twitching with nervous energy. Briggs and Noakes? The loathsome Briggs, and that pretentious little prat Noakes? Shameless opportunists, the pair of them.

Had he known, Richard would certainly have assumed it was about Madrigo, since that was Noakes's only imaginable point of contact with Briggs. His speculations would have included the possibility that the odious Noakes was trying to ensure he received appropriate credit for his tweaking of Richard's 'boring' facade of the building. Or perhaps Richard might have imagined something more treacherous than that: he might have feared that Noakes was hinting at some accommodation of Briggs's money-grubbing attempts either to increase the price of the apartments or to cut corners on their quality. Either of those compromises would represent, to Richard, a denial of the whole point of Madrigo; a tarnishing of its powerful symbolism. As far as Richard could tell, neither Noakes nor Briggs had even the faintest inkling of how significant Madrigo could be for the reputation of Urbanski (to say nothing of Richard's own reputation). 'Revolutionary' would be the word everyone would use, provided the project retained its integrity.

But Richard didn't know they were meeting. He was, at that time, enjoying himself – indulging himself – by tinkering with some amendments to the sketches he had prepared for Lincoln the Hunter's renovations, convivium and all. Since there seemed to be no budgetary constraints, he was beginning to think he should recommend a total demolition and rebuild, after all.

*

'Master Noakes,' said Briggs, rising to meet his young guest. Everyone said Noakes was a wunderkind, but Briggs had seen no evidence of it and saw none now. For an architect, the man seemed to lack any sense of personal style. To Briggs, he looked scruffy, almost unkempt. The man was a wimp, Briggs had concluded, and that rather suited his purposes.

'Ah, Mr Briggs,' said Noakes, adopting the same tone of playful courtliness. Everyone said Briggs was a ruthless monster, but Noakes, so recently humiliated by the experience of being rescued from the waters of Camp Cove by the willowy wife of Richard Brooks, was in a receptive mood: if Briggs wanted to see him, then he certainly wanted to hear what Briggs had to say. The thought of starting his own firm was never far from the mind of Philip Noakes, and his harbour adventure had renewed his enthusiasm for the idea. It seemed likely he would never live down the perception among his Urbanski colleagues that he was a comical – even farcical – figure. Unfortunately, but perhaps inevitably, someone had captured the whole frightful episode on their mobile phone, and the footage had been enthusiastically circulated around the office. People had taken to referring to him as 'Fish-food Phil' – a tasteless reference to the vomiting, he supposed – and one quite junior person had asked him, with a disrespectful smirk, 'Do you think you'd be safer on the ground floor?' Occasionally, as he stepped into the lift, he would hear someone behind him give a muffled shout: 'Man overboard!' Even 'Going down?' seemed to be said with an edge, when someone was holding the lift door for him. The fact that he had been rescued by a *woman* was taken to be a particular sign of weakness. Noakes's attempts to dismiss such comments as sexist failed to convince even the women in the office.

The embarrassment of the event itself now seemed as nothing compared with the persistence of all this childishness. Noakes knew his swift rise to the rank of partner had provoked feelings of jealousy among some of his colleagues, but he had not previously experienced any actual hostility. It was as if his unfortunate accident had provided an excuse for people to unleash their hidden feelings towards him, under the guise of light-heartedness. It was all very tedious.

'I need your advice, Master Noakes.'

This was more like it. This was the level of seriousness Noakes had been hoping for; the level of deference he felt was appropriate to a partner in the firm, no matter how new or how young.

'It's about Freya. That gorgeous woman who plucked you out of the harbour.' As he said this, Briggs couldn't restrain a smile, though he didn't quite laugh.

Noakes's heart sank. What now? He nodded at Briggs.

'I need to be sure of your discretion in this matter,' Briggs went on. 'I think something I did might have been seriously misinterpreted by Freya, and quite possibly by Richard, too.'

Noakes nodded again.

'The thing is, I have the greatest respect for Richard. As I'm sure you do. Everyone does.'

Noakes kept nodding. 'Everyone,' he agreed mournfully.

'The thing is . . . well, look, the thing is, I wrote an email to Freya praising her courage and her skill – you'd agree with that assessment, I'm sure, Master Noakes.'

Noakes said nothing.

'And I invited her to meet me for a drink.'

Noakes's eyebrows rose involuntarily, but he still said nothing.

'I know what you're thinking,' Briggs went on, 'but, you see, the thing is, it actually wasn't like that at all. I really did want to praise her courage. There was no sleazy hidden agenda, I assure you. Well, perhaps a hidden agenda, but not a sleazy one.'

Noakes scarcely knew where to look.

'You think I'm a sleaze? Is that what you mean by that shifty bloody look? You think I wanted to fuck the wife of my architect? *Really?*'

'No, of course not. It's just that . . .'

'Come clean, Master Noakes.'

'Well, the fact that you're raising this with me. I mean, I imagine you can see yourself how a thing like that could be misinterpreted. I mean, I –'

'If you had written to the woman in those terms, it wouldn't have been misinterpreted.'

'Well, I –'

'It was misinterpreted because of prejudice. Sheer bloody-minded prejudice. I'm a developer. You know – a *developer*. So naturally I'm a rapacious bastard in my personal life as well as my business dealings. Isn't that right, Master Noakes? *Rapacious*, wouldn't you say? Is that what you think? Is that what Richard thinks?'

'Of course not.'

'Of course not,' Briggs said, mimicking Noakes unkindly. 'Master Noakes, let me come to the point. I wrote to Freya in the hope of having a quiet conversation with her about Madrigo, and about Richard's blinkered approach to it. I had thought she might be able to raise some of my concerns with him more delicately – more diplomatically – than I seem to be capable of. My wife, God bless her, in the years before I lost her to that well-known wife-stealer called Alzheimer . . . she never hesitated to draw attention to my lack of diplomatic skill. All the subtlety and charm of a pre-fab granny flat, she used to say. The pre-fab granny flat was a sore point between us, but let's not go there.'

Briggs paused and looked away. Noakes was astonished to see a single tear slide down his cheek.

'So, okay,' Biggs said, refocusing, 'I admit I miscalculated. Trying to be subtle. I shouldn't even try. Never works for me. Anyway, that's water under the bridge. Sorry, you probably don't like water metaphors. The thing is, I clearly offended the lovely Freya – or at any rate alarmed her – so that avenue of approach is closed.'

Noakes, meanwhile, sensed an opening. 'Tell me more about your Madrigo concerns.'

'Isn't it obvious? The whole thing has been arse-about from the start. I didn't dream up this development and then go hunting for an architect. Richard dreamed up the project – it's like a personal crusade with him – and then came to me, begging me to finance the thing. As if I'm some kind of fucking philanthropist. Don't get me wrong, Master Noakes – I'm all in favour of stylish, low-cost housing . . . it's just that every job has to be profitable or I'm history. Do you have any idea what it costs to put someone in a halfway-decent nursing home for ten years, with the prospect of another ten or even twenty to come? Any idea? Of course you don't and may you never have to find out. Anyway, I'm a pretty modest developer, in the scheme of things, not some big corporation. It's just me, basically. I take it one job at a time. I budget with great care. I'm less reckless than I might seem to you. Richard latched on to me because he and I have the same approach to that killer combination of beauty and utility, and we pulled off a couple of very nice knock-down-and-rebuilds together. Gave him a sniff.'

'A sniff?'

'He thought I might be a soft touch when it came to his big dream. I like his dream. I *love* his dream. You've seen the concept. You've worked on it, haven't you? Lovely. Terrific. Game-changer. But the margin has to be there or I'm cactus.'

'And?'

'And what?' Noakes was beginning to irritate Briggs. There was something not quite right about all this barely suppressed eagerness.

'It sounds as if you might want me to say the sort of thing to Richard you were hoping to get Freya to say. Am I right?'

'Don't get ahead of yourself, Master Noakes. You're a colleague, not a wife. Totally different approach. Totally different strategy.'

'Of course.'

'Richard's position – Richard's vision – has to be respected.'

'Of course.'

'The thing is, since I wrote that email, there's been a certain awkwardness between Richard and me. A certain tension. I want your help in easing it. I want you to be my Johnny-on-the-spot. Understand?'

'Not exactly.'

'How should I put this? A watching brief. Check the figures. Check the costings. If I have to pull out, I have to pull out.'

'I thought you'd –'

'Already signed on? Nothing is settled. We have a sort of agreement. An understanding. Nothing more.'

'You want me to make my own appraisal of the project?'

Briggs eyed Noakes with increasing distaste. He was beginning to think a direct approach to Richard might be best. But the Freya thing had certainly come between them. And, sure, he had rather relished the prospect of spending an hour with a young and very attractive woman, quite apart from the business in hand.

'Appraisal? Hardly that. But we need to cut down the scale, and Richard doesn't seem to hear me when I say that. I don't want to walk, but I don't want to be the bunny, either. Richard thinks the promise of a plaque on the building will get me over the line. A reasonable profit margin is what will get me over the line. As things stand, the risk is unacceptable.'

'Maybe you should just tell Richard that. Or maybe I could work up some costings for a scaled-down version. Something you can put in front of Richard.'

'Or maybe I've made a big mistake raising this with you. Richard can be a difficult bugger sometimes, but I wonder if you're half the man he is.'

'I'll tell you one thing about Richard.'

'No disloyalty now.'

'No disloyalty.'

'What?'

'He's an admirer of rationality. Logical argument. He's suspicious of emotion – his own and anyone else's. We all know we can win Richard over with the facts, but we'll leave him cold with more woolly attempts at persuasion.'

'Woolly?'

'Fuzzy. More feelings than facts.'

'But I've explained my reservations to him.'

'He needs facts. He needs evidence that Madrigo could still be a standard-bearer without breaking the bank.'

'Curious that a man who, as you say, is suspicious of emotion is so emotionally committed to this thing. That's not entirely rational, is it?'

'I said he was an admirer of rationality. I didn't say he was rational.'

'Say no more, Master Noakes. I think we understand each other.'

Variatio 22. a 1 Clav.

allabreve.

22

Coming Home –
11th Variation –
'An Uncertain Smile'

My favourite homecomings are those when Freya greets me at the door and unleashes her most uninhibited, her most enchanting smile – a smile that lights up her face and melts my heart, every single time.

It's such a welcome contrast from the more usual sight of Freya sitting at the convivium table, hunched over a musical score or tapping away on her tablet. I can't help it: when she sits with her back to the door like that, I am always reminded of that dreadful day when I came home to find my mother in such distress, sitting just like that, hunched just like that, with her shoulders shaking just like that.

Ah, but Freya's smile. Those bright white teeth, perfectly shaped, perfectly spaced; those full lips, generously parted; sparkling eyes, crinkled nose; the single dimple in her right cheek; chin raised, as if she's expecting to be kissed.

And yet, over the years, I've learnt to be wary of that smile.

I've seen her beam it an audience as if she's giving them herself as well as her music, only to have her tell me later she was dying inside because she knew full well the quartet hadn't done their best and she used her smile as a kind of compensation – like the charm of the conman, perhaps, though she didn't put it like that.

I've seen her win her mother over with a smile that seemed utterly conciliatory, only to hear her in the car on the way home fulminating – raging – against her mother's stupidity, or duplicity, or complicity with Fern over some plot to rein in Felicity or, worse, some strategy for getting Mike to toe some line or other. The smile was a weapon, consciously deployed, she seemed to be implying. She knew its power.

The same thing with Daniel – 'winning him back' was how she once put it to me; getting him to see things her way, or at least to accept her way even if he didn't agree with it. Melting his resistance with that smile when she ran out of arguments or patience. Manipulation, pure and simple, and very impressive in its way.

At one level, I couldn't object, could I? Beauty *and* utility. The smile could be a thing of beauty in and of itself, and it could be a device that *worked*. But once I came to understand the way she used that smile, I had more of a sense of its utility than its beauty: it didn't enchant me as it once had; it didn't go straight to my soul, bypassing my brain.

Once that happened, the smile began to worry me, to irritate me – even to unnerve me.

I realise that any 'face that launched a thousand ships' is likely to be a face that sank a thousand others. There's always a shadow.

But I confess to a gnawing sense of disappointment. Not a sudden thing, but a gradual awakening to the idea that I, along with everyone else, had read more – or perhaps less – into that smile than was ever there.

Ever there? Maybe that's unfair. Maybe the smile began its career innocently enough – I've seen it in embryo in photos from her childhood – and only took on this manipulative aspect as it dawned on Freya that she had this magical source of power at her disposal.

The thing is, I'd still rather have it shining on me than not. Even a grin is welcome these days.

23

Lincoln the Hunted

You've called Lincoln the Hunter. Leave a message, and keep living the dream.

'Lincoln, this is Richard Brooks from Urbanski again. I emailed those sketches to you, as you asked, along with our indicative quote. Both very rough – the sketches and the quote. I put hard copies in the post, as well. That package should have reached you last week. I'd be interested in your response. Give us a call when you have a mo.'

You've called Lincoln the Hunter. Leave a message, and keep living the dream.

'Richard Brooks here, Lincoln. No pressure. Just interested to have your reaction to the drawings, and our rough quote, of course. Very rough. I've had one or two further thoughts about the convivium. I really think it could be transformative – not just of the house, but of your whole lifestyle. I'm not exaggerating. For the boys as well as you and Hermione. I'm looking forward to meeting Hermione. I wonder if we could arrange our next meeting at a time when she might be able to join us.'

You've called Lincoln The Hunter. Leave a message, and keep living the dream.

'Richard, again, Lincoln. I'll shoot you an email.'

From: Richard Brooks <rbrooks@urbanski.com.au>
To: Lincoln the Hunter <lincolnthehunter@gmail.com>
Subject: Convivium for you and Hermione

Hi Lincoln,

Just checking you received the concept sketches and our preliminary quote. All subject to detailed discussion and further refinement, of course.

Please call or email, just to confirm that you have received the material, and to indicate when we might next meet. Ideal if Hermione could also be present.

Richard

From: Lincoln the Hunter <lincolnthehunter@gmail.com>
To: Richard Brooks <rbrooks@urbanski.com.au>
Subject: Automatic reply: Convivium for you and Hermione

Thanks for reaching out.

Unavailable this week. All good.

Live the dream!

Lincoln the Hunter

You've called Lincoln The Hunter. Leave a message, and keep living the dream.

'Lincoln, Richard Brooks again. I sent you an email. I'll leave you in peace. I might try to make contact with Hermione through the hospital. I just need a please proceed or a please back off. I hope you're okay.'

*

'St Walburga's Private Hospital. How may I direct your call?'

'Hi. My name is Richard Brooks. I'm trying to reach Dr Hermione Hunter. I understand she works there. I'm doing some architectural work for Dr Hunter and her husband, and I am having difficulty making contact with them. Is there any way you can put me in touch with her?'

'Is this a private call, Richard?'

'Well, yes, it's not medical, if that's what you mean. I'm just wanting to make contact and –'

'She won't respond to non-medical phone messages, but if you leave me an email address, I'll pass it on. I can't promise she'll respond, but I will see she gets the message. Her professional name is Dr Bayley, by the way.'

From: Hermione Bayley <drbayley@stwalburgas.org.au>
To: Richard Brooks <rbrooks@urbanski.com.au>
Subject: Lincoln Hunter

Mr Brooks,

I understand you were trying to contact Lincoln Hunter regarding some architectural matter. I assume that if Mr Hunter wishes to discuss this matter with you, he will know how to reach you.

(Dr) Hermione Bayley

Clients, thought Richard. He once overheard a young teller in the local branch of his bank saying to a colleague: 'All these customers stop us getting on with our work.' He knew what that kid meant. Clients were always the problem. Hunter, vanished; Briggs, wavering. The uncertainty of it; the insecurity.

Thank God for Freya, thought Richard: my rock, my fortress, my solid core. May she never falter.

24

'Would You Ever Leave Him?'

Whenever I meet Fern away from the rest of the family, the conversation almost always becomes either conspiratorial or confessional. When our husbands are present – with or without Fern's two kids – we tend to revert to rather girlish behaviour, teasing each other and even occasionally giggling. It amuses the blokes. When Felicity is present, we tend to be rather stern and defensive. She likes to spend time with us more than we like to spend time with her.

And Mum? Unalloyed adulation is what she expects from us, and what she gets, mostly. Extravagant, hypocritical expressions of admiration and gratitude. It's an unattractive habit, except to Mum, but we've both developed it as a kind of pre-emptive strike. You should hear our little gasps of pleasure at the sight of a new pair of cushions, or a new cashmere pashmina . . . or her new dog. Perhaps we actually enjoy playing the game: it's better than having to defend or explain ourselves all over again. When Mum is present, we even make charitable remarks about each other.

But when it's just us, it feels almost as honest, almost as frank, almost as naked as gazing into a full-length bathroom mirror. Sometimes we eat. Mostly we just drink.

A question we always ask each other is: 'Did you feel like leaving him this week?' It's like a little ritual; a checkpoint; a way into the heart of things. We've been doing it for years. I don't think we ever mean it literally – or not usually. But it's not exactly a joke, either. Ever since high school, Fern has been a fan of Albert Camus, and that question is her own personal version of his assertion: 'There is but one truly serious philosophical problem, and that is suicide.' Fern has never contemplated suicide – and I'm tempted to say she never would – but when she sees a couple destroying their marriage, whether by slow and painful strangulation or by a quick, lethal shock, she regards it as a form of suicide. So she thinks the Camus question applies to any discussion of our marriages.

'If we are our marriage and our marriage is us,' she likes to say, 'then killing it off is a form of suicide.'

Marriage has always been a bigger thing – even a grander thing – to Fern than it has been to me. At least, I think that's true. I admit I was desperate to be married to Richard, just as I've become desperate to have his child, but I don't think I've ever had quite that sense of utterly merged identity that Fern seems to have with Mike. I hope he feels the same. I assume he does. He acts as if he's still devoted, after all these years. I'd call Fern committed rather than devoted, but there you go – I guess there's more to Mike than meets the eye. There's always more to *everyone* than meets the eye.

Except with Richard: I sometimes feel, unkindly, that there's slightly less than meets the eye. I'd never say that to Fern, of course. And there's so much good in Richard – in who he is and especially in what he does. Professionally, I mean. He's a good architect. And he's a good man, too. Don't get me wrong. When I occasionally hanker after something more, I don't even know what I mean by 'more'. More *dangerous*? No, thanks. Richard is safer than he looks, and that's fine by me. Debonair – even dashing – on the outside; pushing the boundaries in his work; yet a frightened little boy inside, I sometimes think.

Anyway, Fern sees the destruction of a marriage as the removal of a big part of your identity: hence the Camus/suicide analogy. She's drawing a long bow, it seems to me, but it's fun to play the game. For Fern, the biggest question of all is: 'What would it take to make you leave him?'

In her own case, there's no question: infidelity would do it. If she found Mike had strayed, she would unhesitatingly commit marriage suicide – and quite possibly homicide, as well, she says.

I mostly go along with that, or I try to sound as if I do. But I'm not so sure. For a start, I'd like to think there was a bit of leeway in a long-haul marriage. Would one indiscretion necessarily sink the whole enterprise? If it coincided with a very serious, very explicit withdrawal of love, perhaps even its replacement by hatred or cold indifference, then sure. But I've always been drawn to the view that if one partner becomes seriously involved with someone else, that is surely a symptom that all was not well anyway. But I know I'm less rigid than Fern about such things. And we're both convinced Mum is less rigid about such things than she lets on, though the straying – if there was any – was her own, not Dad's. Mum is brilliant at talking the talk, but she is capable of walking a very different walk.

Whenever we have these conversations, I wonder what I could possibly say if Richard confessed to having strayed – or if I found out some other way. Would I be up for a reciprocal confession, admitting to those two (or was it three?) mad afternoons when I succumbed to Daniel and found he was just as hopeless as he had been at nineteen? More experienced, of course; less tentative; but no more accomplished. Richard is my gold standard in that department. No question. Ten out of ten for quality, if not for frequency.

I've never said any of this to Fern, though I have chastised her for her lack of generosity and understanding in her hypothetical response to Mike's hypothetical philandering. (Fern is not by nature a forgiver. Neither is Mum. Dad was. I want to be. But I also don't want to be put to the test.) I occasionally ask her to reverse the roles. How would she expect Mike to react to some indiscretion of hers? But she won't go there, though she did once blush when I pressed her.

As far as Fern is aware, Daniel and I remain close friends and professional colleagues. I admit (though never to Fern) that his adoration is sometimes a tonic, but I know it would have become deeply tedious if we had ever lived together year after year: eventually I'd have wanted to slap his silly face. Either that, or he'd have become disillusioned by the reality of being constantly with me, up close. At least Richard has never shown any sign of being disillusioned, though he sometimes lags a bit when it comes to sustaining the adoration.

'Anything else?' I ask her. 'Would anything else drive you to commit marriage suicide?'

She says not, though she did once concede that sexual abuse of their children would cross the line.

'What about drugs? Addiction to internet porn? Squandering the family finances?'

All those things could be dealt with somehow, she claims, with the confidence of someone who's never had to deal with any of them.

'What about boredom?' I've only ever asked this once. She unleashed such a furious attack on that idea, I never mentioned it again. Fern is inclined to a certain inflexibility and she's as inflexible as a dry stick on this point: 'Partners make each other boring. I'm sure of it. I've seen it over and over. If I thought Mike was becoming boring, I'd take a good hard look at myself.' There was more than a hint of warning in it: I had once, when Richard was deeply immersed in a new project, unwisely mentioned to Fern that I feared he could become boring.

Whenever Fern presses me – 'What would make *you* leave?' – I often find myself inwardly melting at the realisation that Richard really is a one-off. A treasure. A lovely, lovely man with some deeply irritating qualities. I admit I have contemplated violence when he has said, for the thousandth time, 'Home is the sailor, home from sea, and the hunter home from the hill,' but otherwise . . .

'Go on, Frey. There must be something. He's already been divorced once, so we know *he's* capable of suicide. What about you?'

I should never have mentioned it, of course. Once these things are out, there's endless scope for teasing or even ridicule.

'He's such a noisy eater, it drives me completely nuts. I sometimes think that could possibly drive me away.'

'You're not serious.'

'Of course I'm not serious. We're playing, aren't we? But I must admit there are times when –'

'Oh my God, you *are* serious! Frey! Noisy eating? Why don't you just put on some background music? A bit of ambient noise?'

I knew it was a mistake to mention it, because it's not the literal fact of the loud chomping, the gulping, the barely suppressed belching, the cutlery on teeth or the clicking jaw, is it? All that is bad enough. But it's what those things signify. It's the lack of sensitivity to . . . well, to me, really. It feels like a demonstration, every single time, that he doesn't get how irritating it is on the surface, or how deeply it offends me. No one who *really* knew me, who *really* loved me, who respected my hyper-sensitivity to sound, would persist with that behaviour. Especially not after I had actually raised it. Of course, I raised it in the form of criticism of him – an attack, really – rather than describing how it made me feel. My therapist has told me I got that totally the wrong way around. (My therapist. That's another thing I don't share with Fern. Fern is not what you'd call psychologically minded. She likes philosophical puzzles, not actual psychodrama.)

Fern persists: 'You don't think you're being a teensy bit neurotic about this, Frey? *I've* never noticed Richard being such a noisy eater that I had to leave the room or anything.'

Better, really, to leave it on the surface and let Fern think I am a bit neurotic. Okay, I *am* a bit neurotic. More than a bit. Who isn't? Of course I would never leave Richard because he's a noisy eater. Of course I wouldn't. But it's that kind of thing – noisy eating, leaving the fridge door open, clapping at the end of the first movement of a work – that could tip you over the edge if other, bigger things were becoming a problem.

Fern wouldn't let it go. 'Why not turn on some music? Isn't that the easiest way out of this? You're the expert. Get the level right and you simply wouldn't hear poor Richard munching away.'

There's another thing which would probably strike Fern as neurotic. I refuse to use music as background noise – whether to mask Richard's rowdy mouth-work or anything else. I also *hate* it when music is used to create an ambience that will encourage people to chatter and, in the process, drown out the music. Music as white noise? Elevator music? Supermarket music? This is the abuse of music. It's the prostitution of art.

Go on, say it: when Continental Drift plays at parties and weddings and conference dinners, we, too, are prostituting our art. Correct. Inconsistent? You bet. We're shamelessly doing it for the money. Just as supermarkets are shamelessly trying to lower shoppers' defences by the very scientific programming of music. It's an awful abuse of the art, because it's so transparently driven by dollars. But if I turned on some music in my own house as a way of disguising my husband's disgusting eating habits, that would be just another form of music-abuse, to my mind.

All I say to Fern is that I hate to think of music being used in such a utilitarian way.

'What about the famous Richard mantra – beauty and utility? Can't music still be beautiful when you're using it for such banal purposes?'

I smile and shrug. 'The bottom line, Fern, is that I'm not leaving him over this. I'm not leaving him period. For a start, I'd have to go back to teaching. Or busking. At my age?'

Most times when we meet, that recurring question – 'Did you feel like leaving him this week?' – doesn't lead us into deep water.

And we don't only talk about men and marriage, of course. That's just a kind of nudge, to get the conversation going and put things into perspective. We long ago agreed that if we didn't feel like leaving our husbands this week, then everything else could be coped with.

Fern juggles two kids, a part-time job, many more visits to Mum than I ever manage, and a marriage that seems to make her and Mike completely happy. I sometimes have to pad out my account of the week to make it seem as if I'm pulling my weight; Fern is a bit like Mum when it comes to music.

Naturally, I told Fern about the harbour rescue episode involving poor Philip Noakes. Naturally, Fern reported it to Mum. Naturally, Fern reported Mum's reaction to me. She was deeply unimpressed. Naturally. That's why I wasn't going to mention it to Mum myself.

So unladylike, she had said, according to Fern; nothing more. I could have predicted that, right down to the tilt of the chin and the almost imperceptible sniff. But Fern and I both knew the real problem: to engage with that story – let alone to actually praise me – would be to risk one of those moments when she might have felt outshone by one of her daughters. In any case, she was always as dismissive of my swimming prowess and my lifesaving qualifications as she was of my music.

I almost wish Fern hadn't told her. But I get sick of saying to Fern, 'Don't mention this to Mum.'

The funny thing is, Mum obviously mentioned it to Flick, who then rang me in a state of high excitement and breathless admiration.

I want to love Flick. I want to be nicer to her. Kinder. I wish I could trust her. I wish she felt more like a sister. The Monk gets in the way of that, which isn't Flick's fault, of course. (I doubt she's ever paused to wonder why 'Uncle Charles' is so nice to her and not to us.) Mum calls Flick her 'freedom child', which I suspect carries even more freight than it appears to. I do envy the way Flick handles Mum so much better than Fern or I seem able to do.

I have a recurring dream about Flick. (I've given up discussing dreams with Fern: she thinks they are merely the drainpipe of the mind, flushing away the day's detritus. I disagree.) In this dream, I'm swimming in very deep, very murky water and Flick emerges from beneath me, her arms stretching towards me and that red hair streaming behind her like a mermaid's. She is pleading: 'Don't leave me.' Over and over. Even though we're underwater, I can hear her voice clearly: plaintive, haunting. I usually wake from that dream sobbing. Fortunately, Richard never hears me. Deep and peaceful sleep is one of his many accomplishments.

Would I ever leave Richard? I know he fears that very thing, and I wish I could find the words to convince him that it will never happen. This is a strange kind of love we have, but maybe no stranger than any other kind of love. Sometimes I think the gaps between us are like unbridgeable chasms; sometimes I think they are mere fissures. I fear I could become a very unpleasant person if I didn't have Richard in my life.

25

Coming Home –
12th Variation – 'A Visit
from Angelina'

The sight of his convivium gladdened Richard's heart, as it always did when he came home (in spite of the clichéd flooring), but the gladness was short-lived.

Seated at the farmhouse table were Freya, with her back to him, and Angelina, the progeny of his disastrous first marriage. Angelina, now twenty-six years old, was precisely the age Freya had been when Richard first met her. He tries not to dwell on that fact.

To make matters worse, the two women were laughing in a way that seemed to Richard, coming suddenly upon them, to be somewhat conspiratorial. (He would never know what had amused them, of course. If he asked Freya later, how could he trust whatever answer she gave? He might be a slow learner in such matters, but he was making progress.)

Freya turned to face him, and both women let their laughter subside into warm smiles.

'Hello, my darling,' said Freya, to Richard's surprise and her own. She never greeted him with a term of such endearment when they were alone, though she couldn't explain why. She stopped short of 'How was your day?', though.

'Hi, Dad,' said Angelina, also to Richard's surprise. He never really thought of himself as a father, and was always slightly shocked when he heard Angie's voice on the phone – now the voice of a mature woman – calling him Dad. It was slightly easier hearing it from her in person, though he couldn't explain why.

It was possible that Freya had mentioned Angie was coming tonight. It was also possible that she hadn't. It was perfectly possible that this was an unannounced visit, or the result of a last-minute exchange of texts with Freya. Angie now worked in Melbourne as a travel agent and made frequent trips to Sydney, often at short notice, and she had taken to calling in whenever she had a free evening.

Richard bent and kissed each woman in turn, Freya on the lips, Angie on the cheek.

'How has your day been?' asked Angie, as if this were a routine homecoming, a standard domestic ritual. Or perhaps as if Richard were a client of her travel agency.

'Oh.' Richard hesitated. It had been a particularly difficult day. Briggs still seemed reluctant to give final approval to Richard's plans for Madrigo, although Richard had believed it was virtually a done deal a week ago. No one but Richard himself – and certainly not Briggs – had any idea how important Madrigo was to him. 'Fine. Thanks.'

'Gosh. That sounded pretty unconvincing.'

Between meetings with his daughter, Richard always forgot how direct Angie could be. It was an unwelcome echo of her mother, though he acknowledged that Angie was a far nicer person than she. In fact, between meetings, he tended to forget what a nice person she had become. His groans whenever Freya told him that Angie would be calling in were reflexive, rooted in the past, rather than fair and reasonable, based on more recent experience.

Anyway, here she was – a very pleasant, very confident young woman, apparently unbowed by the burden of their shared history. And he was, after all, still her father. There was no getting around that.

'We thought we might go out for something to eat,' said Freya, and for a moment Richard thought she meant just her and Angie. He was initially offended, then relieved, then aware that he was mistaken. The three of them were apparently going together to 'a little place in Glebe' that Angie knew about.

'My shout,' said Angie, and that surprised both Richard and Freya. 'I have some news.'

Freya glanced at Richard and silenced his question with a slight frown and a quick shake of the head.

'Lovely,' she said to Angie. 'Do you want to come back here to sleep, or will you stay in town?'

'No – I wouldn't inflict that on you. Think of the morning. I'm already installed at my hotel.'

This felt to Richard like a rather off-key exchange, as if the spontaneity was a little staged. He even wondered if the visit had been set up some days ago. Then he wondered if he were becoming paranoid. And then he decided it didn't matter either way. Here she was. And he was still her father.

Freya fed Rondo. Richard went upstairs to change into something more casual. Angie mooched into the living room, flopped into an armchair and scrolled through her messages.

After a few minutes, they reassembled and piled into Freya's Alfa.

'So,' said Angie, after their meals had been served and the small talk was out of the way. Richard noticed that Angie was prefacing many of her sentences with 'so' these days.

'I said I had some news. It's big news actually. Couldn't be bigger.'

Richard and Freya looked at each other, both processing the same set of assumptions, supported by Angie's refusal of wine.

'So Al and I are pregnant.'

'*Both* of you?' said Richard, before he could check himself.

'Oh, Dad,' said Angie, too happy to be irritated.

'That's wonderful news,' said Freya, scarcely able to control the maelstrom suddenly swirling within. So easy for them. Just like that! She kept a smile on her face, as broad as she could manage. 'When?'

'Pretty close to Christmas. Not ideal, I realise. But these things don't always go according to plan.'

Indeed they do not, thought Freya.

'Actually,' Angie said with a giggle, 'we were a bit surprised by this. It's not exactly unplanned, but certainly unexpected.'

Too much information, thought Richard.

She's bragging about her fertility, thought Freya. Okay, so she came off the pill and *bingo*! Very clever.

This doesn't feel as warm as I expected, thought Angie.

'How does Al feel about it?' said Richard, struggling for something to say that might sound solicitous.

'Oh, Al's over the moon. He's already drawing up lists of names.'

'Avoid names beginning with A,' said Richard, managing to mystify both women equally. 'And go for a short name.'

'What? Why?'

'Well ... Angelina, Alexander ... isn't that enough four-syllable names beginning with A for one family?' He sensed he had lost his audience.

'You're well, obviously,' said Freya, trying to calm herself. 'Glowing, in fact. We should have guessed!'

You're glowing, and *you're* not pregnant, Richard was thinking to himself. At least I hope you're not. *Surely* not.

'There's more.'

'What, twins?' Richard asked.

Richard really is in a strange mood, thought Freya.

'No, no. Nothing like that. This is not IVF, Dad.'

Don't rub it in, thought Freya.

'So, Al and I are moving to Sydney. We'll be here before the baby is born. He's got a promotion that involves a transfer, and I've already started talking to Sydney travel agencies. We'll rent something around here – Glebe, Annandale – so we'll practically be neighbours.' Angie said this with a lilt.

'This is all very exciting, I must say,' said Freya, quite pleased to be living even as far away as Birchgrove; too far from Glebe to walk there and back with a pram.

'Al says having grandparents around is so important for the baby's sense of emotional security. You know, being part of a family? And what with Al's dad having passed and his mother being so unwell ... and of course Mum and Fitzy are basically going to travel for the next few years. They're talking about semi-settling in Bali?' A little frown; almost a pout. When she became earnest, Angie sometimes reverted to her teenage habit of giving statements the cadence of questions. 'Mum doesn't actually seem as pleased as I thought she'd be? She even said she's not ready to be a grandmother. Came right out and said it? I bet she'll change her tune when the baby arrives. But, whatever, they won't be living in Sydney. Mum says she can't bear the place?'

As this monologue wound on, Richard found himself trying to imagine being a grandfather. Freya found herself calculating how long it would take Angie to bring up the subject of child care. She would need to understand, right from the start, that Richard and Freya were fully committed to their careers. It was Angie's and Al's baby – not theirs. (But where *was* theirs?)

Richard's first wife will become a grandmother, whether she likes it or not, thought Freya. No hiding place for her. Or for Richard, God help him. But me? I won't be anyone's grandmother. The child has two grandmothers already. Step-grandmother? Me? At my age? And with no baby of my own?

Freya excused herself and went to the washroom, where she looked in the mirror at this potential step-grandmother who so desperately wanted to be an actual mother, no matter how complicated the process. But all she saw were the tears rolling down her cheeks.

Later, in bed, Richard said: 'Looks as if we're going to have a baby around the house, after all.'

'Don't you mean two babies, Richard?'

'Come on, Frey. Can't we drop that? Especially now.'

'The lovely Dr Costa awaits your call. She'll handle everything. Just say the word.'

26.

Variatio 26. a 2 Clav.

26

A Letter from Mother

Wentworth NSW
1 May 1977

My dear little Richie,

Forgive me, I know you're not little – far from it – fifteen
in a few months – almost a man! But you'll always be 'dear
little Richie' to me.

Things have not gone well for me, but that's no reason
why they can't go well for you. I am very proud of you,
and I want you to do your very best at everything you do.
When I think of that wonderful school and those lovely
friends you have – Russell and Geoff and that other one – I
know this is the right thing to do.

This is no place for you out here – or for me, I realise.
Uncle Eric and Aunty Iris have been very kind, but they
have their own life here – their friends and their church
and everything – and I don't really fit in with any of that.
I feel like a fish out of water, to be honest. Nowhere feels
right for me now.

The job Uncle Eric lined up for me hasn't worked out.
Uncle Eric has promised me that he will keep paying
Grandma Davis for your board, so I can relax about that
and so can you. He will include pocket money for you.
I haven't always been fair to Uncle Eric, but he has been a
good husband to Aunty Iris and she says he is a good father
to their girls when they come home for the holidays. He
will be a good uncle to you.

Uncle Eric will keep you informed of eventualities. I am enclosing a photo of you and me on that last ferry ride we had.

There's a poem I want you to read. Grandma Davis might have it in a book of poetry in that little bookcase in her sewing room. Or you could definitely find it in the school library. It's called 'Requiem', by Robert Louis Stevenson. I want you to read it slowly, especially the line, where it says: 'Here he lies where he long'd to be'. Where he *long'd* to be! Isn't that a wonderful thought? Peace at last.

Much love,
Mother x

27

If Only . . .

If only Richard would share more. He's a dear person in many ways, but so, so stitched up. When I catch little glimpses of his life before he met me, my heart is often torn. And yet I want to shake him. Why won't he open up? Why won't he share? His mother's letter, for instance. He has kept that letter from me for twelve years of marriage and only brought it out when I finally snapped over his endless, endless 'home is the sailor' ritual. Once I read the letter, it changed everything, of course. Now I feel like joining in (though I won't – he'd be too self-conscious). Richard was only fourteen when he received that letter, and I think he was simply dazed by the whole episode. I asked him why he didn't ring his mum in Wentworth, but apparently he felt Grandma Davis wouldn't want him to use the phone . . . it's hard to imagine what life was like back then. I wasn't even born when Richard's world fell apart. He still thinks the letter was ambiguous – surely he can see now that it was a suicide note. I guess he doesn't want to face it. He claims he doesn't really know what happened to his mother. He didn't go to the funeral; he's not even sure there was one. And he simply refuses to talk about his father. I assume he's dead, too, by now.

If only I had paid more attention to my mother's letter. I waited far too long to show it to Freya and I must admit I was shocked by her reaction. She was very sympathetic – don't get me wrong. She is basically a very sympathetic person, even though she can be quite acerbic. But she just immediately concluded my mother had committed suicide and wanted to know why I had never told her. She assumed I had always known and been too ashamed to tell her, or whatever. Actually, I had not known, and I still don't know. The whole thing remains shrouded in mystery. At the time, Grandma Davis – never what you would call an *open* woman – froze right up and said how sad it was, and how we must make the best of it. Looking back, that seems a bit cold – a bit weird, even. But she *was* weird. She was my mother's step-mother and only came onto the scene when my mother was a teenager, so perhaps they were never close. I admit I was already getting a bit tired of 'making the best of it' in Grandma Davis's appallingly oppressive house, though I stuck it out until the end of year twelve, when my father's second wife found me digs in a student hostel near the university. It took Freya to point out to me that the date of my mother's death, according to the notice in the local paper sent to me by Uncle Eric – which I had also kept – was the same as the date on the letter. So she died the day she wrote it. Whether by her own hand or not, who knows? Frey certainly thinks so. Frey thinks we should take a trip out to Wentworth to find my mother's grave, possibly visit Uncle Eric in his nursing home. Closure, she says. I don't know. I was more attached to my mother's sister Iris than to Eric, but she died not long after my mother did. It was all a long time ago. I got over it. I'm a very different person now. I need to be.

If only I could bring myself to tell Richard about my weekly sessions with Megan. He's never home during the day so he doesn't know I sneak off every Thursday morning to see her. (Why did I say 'sneak off'? I'm not ashamed of it. It's just that, for some reason, I can't tell

Richard, even though I'd expect to be told if he was seeing a thera-
pist.) If he rang on the landline, he'd assume I was at rehearsal or
a meeting, off for my daily swim, or maybe just shopping. Even if
he was here when I went out, he wouldn't pry. He's interested in
what I do, but he doesn't ever pry. I just wish I had told him in the
beginning. I don't know . . . it would be an awkward conversation.
He would think it was all about him, and it isn't all about him.
*Well, not **all** about him. It is about him, and it's about Daniel,*
and the whole Baby Question, and Angelina moving to Sydney and
bringing her baby right into the middle of our lives, and my mother
being unable to cope with what Felicity has become – symbolised by
her ratty new name, Duskia – and Mum and Richard never quite
managing to relax with each other. Oh, and it's about Fern and
Mike and their two distressingly adorable children . . . and of course
it's about the quartet and what will become of us, and what will
become of me. Is it going to be such a struggle professionally forever?
I know Richard would be hurt if he thought there was this great long
list of things I needed to talk about that I couldn't talk about with
him. Well, I do talk about them with him, but he's a solutions man.

If only I could be more open with Frey. But, as she herself says, it
takes two to tango. I sometimes find her quite secretive, in fact;
quite evasive.

If only Richard were more like Daniel. More open and demonstra-
tive and, well . . . passionate, I guess.

If only Freya could relax and accept that we have a pretty solid life together. I'd say this was a good marriage. This is not a bad way to live. We have friends. We both have jobs we love. We have a house that anyone would be proud to live in, let alone to own. But there's always this sense in Frey that there must be something more, something more . . . something just out of reach.

If only Daniel were more like Richard. More in control of himself. More responsible. More reliable. And, to be honest, a bit better at what he does. I think his future lies in arranging, not performing.

If only I had kissed Angelina. No, not my daughter; the girl I took to the year ten formal. (My daughter is named after her, though her mother never knew why I was so keen on that name.) I remember being amazed when she said she'd come with me. It was all arranged through a friend. She was a spectacularly beautiful girl, but I'm afraid I was an emotional mess at that point in my life. My parents and everything, plus the whole puberty thing – the agony of concealing erections that came unbidden, especially in the presence of someone like Angelina. There's no way I could have risked the embarrassment of pressing myself against her. Better not even to attempt a kiss. But if only I had, I might have been spared the humiliation of everyone finding out that I hadn't. I thought it rather cruel of her to let that be known.

*

197

If only I had never slept with Daniel. He thinks that gives him the right, forever more, to a special kind of intimacy with me. The truth is, Daniel was hopeless in bed. We were both very young and totally inexperienced, of course. But even so.

If only Briggs hadn't developed this thing about Freya. It started when he watched her diving for Philip's shoe and then scrambling back onto the boat. Her undies were saturated, of course, and practically transparent. I didn't like everyone seeing that, but I expected a bit of discretion. Averted eyes. None of that from Briggs, though. 'That woman has a bottom like a peach,' he said when he saw her in the water, before he'd discovered she was my wife. Why did he have to choose those particular words? Then writing to her. My fault. I gave him her email address – what else could I do when he asked in the way he did? I just hope he doesn't push her any further, or she'll react very badly. The tragedy is, Madrigo has lost a lot of its appeal to me now. Knowing what's going on in Briggs's mind, the dream has turned to ashes, rather. I guess he won't pull out, and all the design work is done, so it will still be a fabulous project, but I find I've lost heart. I don't want anything to do with Briggs or his money, yet I'm stuck with it. Amazing how one thing like this can change your perspective so radically. I hadn't realised my attachment to Freya was so *protective* until this happened. It reinforced that Freya means everything to me. To say she's my top priority would be to suggest, mistakenly, that there is any remotely comparable priority. Does 'protective' ever feel to her like 'possessive'? I hope not, though I can see there's a fine line there.

If only Richard had backed me up when I told Briggs, as politely as possible, to keep his hands to himself. I did not appreciate having my bum patted by that sleaze, on the pretext of helping to dry me off. And then, to make matters worse, asking Richard for my email address – 'I want to write and tell her how much I admire her guts' – and Richard gives it to him! So then the whole pathetic ritual. An apparently harmless, admiring email and a minimally polite response from me. Then a wish that we might have a drink sometime so he could tell me in person. A polite rejection by me. Then an apologetic follow-up – I must have misinterpreted his intentions – and a one-liner from me assuring him, with a neat touch of ambiguity, that I had not. Richard, meanwhile, hovering anxiously. Not anxious about what might transpire between Briggs and me – he knows I'm not an idiot – but anxious about how this might affect the Madrigo deal. I expected more credit from Richard for being so restrained. Under any other circumstances, I'd have been brutal.

If only Freya could keep things in perspective. Things play on her mind. It can go on for weeks.

If only Felicity – who is absolutely insisting we all call her Duskia – were not so determinedly feral. She drives Mum to distraction. Fern is more tolerant than I am, but even she is beginning to lose patience. The woman is in her thirties now, for God's sake. The latest thing is Free Love. She is the very first person in the history of the universe to have concluded that pair bonding is a sensible arrangement for the nurture of children but that marriage as an institution is oppressive, repressive, anachronistic, the product of a male supremacist culture and just plain unnatural. Humans are not actually built for monogamy. Good one, Duskia. (I find that name really hard to say, especially to her face.)

If only Freya's mother had managed to warm to me. Don't get me wrong, she's very polite and friendly, but there's some deep reserve there. I know I'm not imagining it. Something held back. She still seems, rather weirdly in my view, to hold that little shit Daniel up as if he's some kind of paragon. Always asking after him and his wretched baby. And the vapid Lizzie. Am I to be compared with *that?* And she enjoys an extraordinary level of intimacy in her relationships with Fern and Freya. I don't know much about the mothers of girls, or how they operate. I guess I don't know much about mothers, period. Angelina's mother was no shining example, I can tell you. And I simply don't know what to think about my own. But I do wonder if there is such a thing as adult mothers and daughters being *too* close. I also wonder whether age is a factor in all this. I am fifteen years older than Frey, and only eight years younger than her mother. Her father was quite a bit older than her mother – these things are very complicated. I'm no psychologist, but maybe her mother is thinking of all the years Frey will be alone after I'm dead, or maybe she's thinking I'm simply too old for her fresh, pure, lovely young Freya. Well, thirty-nine is not *that* fresh; not *that* young. The way Duskia – the sister formerly known as Felicity – is turning out, their mother is understandably inclined to focus on Fern and Frey for her maternal gratification. And she's a very devoted grandmother to Fern's kids, so there's another thing. I can imagine a whole new set of tensions between her mother and me if Frey and I were to have a child, whether conceived right here in our bed or in a Petri dish sitting in some lab on the other side of the world.

If only Mum could take to Richard a bit more wholeheartedly. It breaks my heart to see him yearning for a mother-in-law who could almost be a surrogate mother. I don't know why she holds back. I do know she's got this strangely lingering thing about Daniel and me. But I suspect something murkier. I've discussed it with Fern, who says she really doesn't want to know, even though she's the one who worked out who Felicity's father could be, if it wasn't Dad. I've discussed it with my therapist, of course, and she remains appropriately tight-lipped. Not a flicker of interest from the old Megan, except in the question of why I'm so interested. (Why wouldn't I be interested?) Anyway, Fern the sleuth calculates the freckle-faced chief suspect is about eight years younger than Mum. He drives a green Jag, apparently. Fern actually thinks Mum might be seeing him again. Nothing wrong with that – Dad's long gone. If it's true, Mum is certainly giving nothing away. But is that eight-year gap an unfortunate coincidence that makes her feel awkward around Richard? Her boyfriend the same age as her daughter's husband? Who knows? It's probably just the Daniel thing. Or maybe she simply doesn't like Richard, which would be weird. Everyone likes Richard. There's usually a nice one in a marriage, and he's the nice one in ours.

*

If only Freya wouldn't persist in this fantasy that I am going to drop into some so-called fertility clinic, wank into a jar, and then let a total stranger whisk my sperm off to parts unknown where it will fertilise the egg of some hapless student who's strapped for cash and then have the embryo implanted in the womb of an even more desperate woman who is apparently prepared to walk around for nine months with someone else's foetus inside her, give birth, and then get on with her life as if nothing's happened. Or maybe go through it all again. I admit I don't understand people's motivations for agreeing to do such things. Is it the money? Is it altruism? I have no moral objection to it; I just don't feel inclined to clamber aboard that particular production line myself. I know Freya thinks there should be more passion in our lives – well, what could be *less* passionate than high-tech baby farming? Young couples who are infertile for some reason, but desperate to have their own child – sure. Fine. No problem. But that's not us. Not at our stage of life. If Freya discovers she is pregnant by natural means, I'll be right there in support, every step of the way. But I think I'm pretty safe.

If only I was better at reproduction. Of course, if I were, I might still be stuck with Dave and our children. No, that would never have happened. I would have left him in the middle of one of our cyclonic depressions. Mum was right about Dave. But a baby might well be the thing that's missing from my life with Richard. Richard says he doesn't want another child, and I agree it would be hard for him now, at fifty-four, to face life with a newborn in the house . . . although, come to think of it, Dad must have been a good deal older than that when Felicity was born. (Ah, the Mystery of the Red Hair. No mystery at all, really.)

If only I was better at the personal stuff. I know what's required – I'm not a fool. Frey says there is a deep well of something or other inside me – empathy, perhaps – that hasn't yet been tapped. Look, I'm not unsympathetic to people's various difficulties and traumas – Freya's in particular – though I think such things are often overplayed. I do believe in getting on with life, as far as possible. In that respect, I think architects are a bit like surgeons. You think about that moment when a surgeon wields a scalpel and actually makes an incision in the skin and opens up the body. There's a particular level of self-confidence needed for that. A particular ability to put aside all your natural inclination not to do it and just get on with it. I find that admirable. And I wouldn't expect a surgeon who had that ability to focus on the technical process to be necessarily so terrific at the bedside-manner thing. Most people aren't good at everything. I'm not equating architecture with surgery, but there is a certain amount of bravado involved in both. You're going to build something out of nothing – something very substantial and very permanent. You're going to fill a hole in a streetscape in a very particular way. Size. Shape. Style. You're in the business of *changing people's environment* and that means changing the way they live. A new place in which to live or work, a new space for them to move through. This is actually mind-blowing, if you think about it. A very smart woman at one of our Socially Aware Architects seminars said that if she wanted to improve the life of a community, to raise its moral tone, she'd look for ways to bring people together more, to increase their sense of connectedness. So she'd consult architects and urban planners before she'd bother with moral philosophers or social psychologists. You can't achieve that sense of belonging online, not with the same immediacy, the same three-dimensional intensity. You have to pass people in the street or the corridor, or chat to them at a dog park, or sit with them in a coffee shop or beside a pond. Someone has to create *spaces* that will facilitate this sort of unplanned social interaction. Well, you need to be pretty bold to take that on. You need some of the self-confidence of that surgeon if you're prepared to accept the responsibility of shaping people's lives. Maybe you're going to demolish an eyesore or an inefficient building – like cutting out a tumour – and you're going to replace ugliness with beauty. Alright, maybe you're not always going to be as sensitive to every little nuance in your own personal relationships as some people might want you to be. (Can you have everything? Can you *be* everything?) Do I want to change the world? Yes. Do I want to change Freya? No. Does Freya want to change me? Yes.

If only Richard were not so verbose. His default position is to talk but not to share. I once accused him of approaching every question with an open mouth.

If only Freya understood that my architecture is just as import-ant to me as her music is to her. No – that architecture *is* just as important as music.

If only something would happen. I might have to go back to teaching, though I really don't want to do that. And, to give him his due, Richard doesn't expect me to. My never having to teach again was one of the loveliest offers he made in the very beginning.

If only I hadn't dragged Freya along on that harbour cruise; if only I hadn't invited Briggs. But Santori was mightily impressed by the rescue, so he pays more attention to me now than he ever did before, which is actually not all that welcome. And Philip Noakes is a changed man in his attitude to me. Quite pathetic, really. Apparently I'm not boring anymore. He's suddenly respect-ful again, the way he used to be when he first joined the firm. Now he's suggesting regular breakfast meetings so he can run his work by me and – get this – receive the benefit of my wisdom and experience. He's still a pretentious little prat. *And* now he seems to think that being rescued by my wife entitles him to start hanging around my workspace – I'm almost tempted to call it snooping – and calling me 'Rich'.

If only Richard were as keen, as attentive, as he was in the beginning. It sometimes feels as if marrying me was a project he managed like all his other projects. And he did manage it brilliantly, from the founda-tions up. Now he can just live in it and admire his handiwork. No, that's not fair. What am I trying to say? I don't expect the falling-in-love kind of passion to last, but I still wish there was more passion in our life together. We are each passionate about our work, but we don't seem to be equally passionate about the marriage. I sometimes wonder if Richard has the talent for marriage. I sometimes wonder if I do myself. But maybe it's like being a musician — it's not just the talent, it's the sheer bloody hard slog. Perhaps I should encourage him to think of us as a work in progress. 'Marriage under construc-tion'. That could appeal to him, actually. I might erect a sign.

If only you could draw up plans and specifications for a marriage. Still, I've never created a perfect building, either. But we go on. We get better at it.

If only I could simply accept that what I have with Richard is really quite special compared with the fate of so many other women I know. Richard does love me. And I only hate him intermittently. It reminds me of working on a piece of music — you play the same thing over and over and eventually you either get so heartily sick of it you abandon it, or you get better at it and start to love it more deeply, or perhaps in different ways. We will go on. We will get better at it.

28

Coming Home

The sight of his convivium gladdened Richard's heart, as it always did when he came home, though he could already see a polished concrete floor in his mind's eye. Freya was sitting at the farmhouse table they had imported from France, with her back to him. Richard thought her shoulders gave a little shiver as he entered the convivium, but she appeared to be bent over her iPad, so perhaps she was merely responding to something on the screen.

'Home is the sailor, home from sea, and the hunter home from the hill,' he said, removing his linen jacket and draping it carefully over the back of a chair.

His wife looked up at him and smiled. 'Hello, sailor,' she said.

'You okay, Frey?' Richard asked as he kissed the top of her head.

'I'm fine. Why do you ask?'

'I thought I saw a bit of a shiver as I came in. Can I fetch you a sweater?'

'No, I'm fine. It's not cold. Would you like a drink? Or tea? Have you eaten?'

'Yes. Well, no, not really. I had a late lunch with Briggs. I probably drank more than I should have, but so did he. The food was good.'

'Where did you eat?'

'Beppi's. Where else?'

'So, do you want something to eat?'

Freya, Richard now noticed, was bent not over her iPad but over a score that was covered in pencil marks. He knew what to say.

'No, you're busy. I'll get myself something. Can I get you anything?'

'I'm fine. I ate earlier. Daniel and I had a bite to eat straight after the rehearsal.'

Freya paused, waiting to see if Richard would ask how the rehearsal had gone, how the work was coming on, or even how Daniel was coping with a new baby in the house. Nothing.

She said: 'There's some lasagne in the fridge. You could heat it up in a couple of minutes. I'm happy to heat it while you change, if you like.'

Freya was wearing the long black skirt she sometimes wore to rehearsals. Richard loved the look of her in it. He loved the silky feel of it. His wife – his *young* wife, he often thought with gratitude – was an endless source of aesthetic and sensual pleasure.

He placed his hands on her shoulders, and she turned to face him. He pulled her out of her chair and embraced her, reaching down to stroke the curve of her hips through the thin fabric of her skirt. She responded with a warm kiss.

They stepped apart and smiled at each other.

'I'll heat the food and pour us both a glass of something,' Freya said.

Richard had to admit – but only to himself – that he enjoyed the idea of Freya preparing his food. He particularly enjoyed the sound of her busying herself in the kitchen when he came home from work. He supposed it was a throwback to something quite primitive. Whatever.

Returning to the table, they raised and clinked their glasses of red wine. 'Cheers!' said Richard. '*Salute!*' said Freya. Richard sat and ate his lasagne while Freya continued to work on the score.

After a few minutes, Freya picked up her glass and the score, excused herself, and retreated to her studio. Through the closed door, Richard could hear the rich, resonant sound of her violin and he reflected, yet again, on what a lucky man he was. Freya was beautiful, talented, successful, far less demanding than the wives of most of his friends – he heard regular horror stories from two of his partners at work – *and* she loved him. It sometimes seemed too good to be true, but he believed it *was* true.

Richard often said to his clients that everything in your home – everything in your life – should be either beautiful or useful, or both. He would never say so to Freya, but, to him, she had always fallen squarely into the 'both' category. On top of everything else, she had a bottom like a peach, played the violin like an angel and had a voice like smoke. He used to compliment Freya on her beautiful hair – a fine, greyish gold that hung loosely about her shoulders – until she pointed out that this was a matter of genetics, not accomplishment, and therefore not deserving of praise. 'Handsome is as handsome does' was one of her favourite aphorisms.

Forty-five minutes later, Freya emerged from her studio and announced that Rondo needed to be taken outside for a pee and a short walk. She offered to do it and asked Richard if he would like to come too.

He glanced at his watch. 'I think I'll get ready for bed, if you don't mind. Early start.'

'That's fine.' Freya ran upstairs to the bedchamber and changed into tracksuit pants and a sweater. At the sound of her taking the leash off the hook on the back of the laundry door, Rondo, asleep on the floor of the convivium, sprang to life and scrambled to the front door, his paws slipping and sliding on the pavers, the tail wagging the dog.

Richard checked his emails, sorted some papers for the morning, brushed his teeth and got into bed. He read for a few minutes, felt drowsy, and rolled onto his side.

When Freya returned, Richard was snoring lightly. She smiled, undressed, and slipped into bed beside him. She, too, read until drowsiness overwhelmed her.

Acknowledgements

Given the structure of *The Question of Love*, my primary debt is, of course, to Johann Sebastian Bach. Countless other composers – and jazz musicians – have employed the 'theme and variations' form, but Bach remains the exemplar.

I am grateful to Ingrid Ohlsson, my publisher at Pan Macmillan, for supporting my attempt to adapt the musical form to the written word, and to Ariane Durkin for creating the book's 'architecture' and guiding the project to fruition. Ingrid and Ariane have been ably supported by creative editor Naomi van Groll, and editorial assistant Belinda Huang.

Ali Lavau has brought her characteristically sensitive editing skills to the project, having offered constructive advice at an early stage of the book's development and thoughtful criticism of the final draft. Rebecca Hamilton's proofreading included valuable editorial input. I also wish to acknowledge Kane Shepherd's creativity and sensitivity in typesetting the book, and Alissa Dinallo's beautiful cover design.

My wife, Sheila, has lived with the project through the years of its evolution, offering both criticism and encouragement, and I am grateful, as ever, for her loving support.